INFERNO

PART 3

USA TODAY BESTSELLING AUTHOR

T.K. LEIGH

INFERNO: PART 3

Published by Carpe Per Diem, Inc. / Tracy Kellam, 25852 McBean Parkway # 806, Santa Clarita, CA 91355

Edited by: Kim Young, Kim's Editing Services

Quotes from *The Divine Comedy* by Dante Alighieri, Rev. H.F. Cary translation (1814).
Quotes from *The Taming of the Shrew* by William Shakespeare (1592).
Quotes from *Henry VI* by William Shakespeare (1595).
Quotes from *Macbeth* by William Shakespeare (1623).
Quotes from *As You Like It* by William Shakespeare (1623).
Quotes from *Julius Caesar* by William Shakespeare (1623).
Quotes from *Letters of Abelard and Hèlöise* by Peter Abelard and Hèlöise (1722).
Quotes from *A Midsummer Night's Dream* by William Shakespeare (1600).

Cover Design: Dana Leah, Designs by Dana
Cover Image Copyright kiuikson 2018
Used under license from Shutterstock.com

To Stan and Harper Leigh… *Sempre e per sempre…*

FLAME

There is no greater grief than to remember days
Of joy, when misery is at hand.
- Dante Alighieri, *The Divine Comedy*
Inferno, Canto V

CHAPTER ONE

ONE FOOT IN FRONT of the other. That was all I had to do. One step at a time. It was what the coin…*fate* told me I should do. Judging from the past ten days, I knew in my heart fate was real, that she wouldn't steer me wrong, that this was all part of her plan.

Then why was there a sick taste in my mouth about what would happen once I left the security area of the airport? What would life be like? Would it be the same as it was before? Was I making a huge mistake?

When I reached the sign warning me there would be no re-entry once I passed, I hesitated. I looked from where I'd come to where I was headed. Both held uncertainty. Was one choice better than the other? Was one path *easier* than the other? I couldn't be sure. All I knew was I'd tossed a coin. I had to believe fate knew what she was doing when she showed me which direction to take.

Hardening myself for whatever awaited me on the other side, I sucked in a long breath and walked through a pair of sliding glass doors, my heels clicking on the tile. There was no turning back now. But was this where I truly belonged?

I immediately came to a stop, closing my eyes and

holding my breath, almost expecting something horrible to happen as fate's way of telling me I'd misread her signs. But nothing did. No big explosion. No bolt of lightning hitting me. No swarm of locusts. Life carried on, hurried travelers passing me as they sought the comfort of their homes or hotel rooms.

Refocusing ahead of me, I continued up the ramp, the fluorescent lights overhead feeling as if they were burning my skin. I scanned the crowd, watching old friends hugging after not seeing each other for any given length of time. I couldn't help but feel like this was all wrong, like I was a stranger here, like the coin had steered me wrong. Maybe I should have followed my heart instead.

"Ellie!" Mila's voice cut through the bustle of bodies. I snapped my head to the left.

The instant I saw her tall, slender frame rushing toward me, I exhaled, dropping my bags and walking into her arms. It wasn't until this moment that reality sank in. I'd actually gotten on that plane and returned home to the pieces of a broken life. I didn't want to be here, but I wasn't sure Rome was the answer, either. I didn't know *what* the answer was. All my life, I'd always had a plan. Now I was lost, a fish swimming upstream against a current, getting nowhere.

"I really hoped I wouldn't see you here today," Mila lamented, rubbing my back. Her own voice sounded as pained as I felt.

"It's for the best," I struggled to respond through the lump in my throat, pulling out of her arms as I swiped

2

away the few tears that had escaped.

Squeezing my biceps, she peered at me with comforting green eyes. "Why did you come back?"

"Why wouldn't I?" I shook off what she was insinuating. "I had a round-trip ticket."

She shrugged. "So? That doesn't mean anything."

"Mila," I sighed, my shoulders falling. "I don't want to talk about it right now. Like I told you earlier in the week…" I grabbed the handles of my bags, rolling them toward the automatic doors leading to the busy pick-up area of the airport. "It was just a vacation fling." My voice faltered. Nothing could be further from the truth. I didn't want to rehash everything I'd felt, everything I'd experienced with Dante. The wound was still too raw, the ache in my chest still too painful, the memory of his skin on mine still too real. "Nothing more," I finished, the words barely audible.

"Whatever you need to tell yourself, Ellie. I won't beat it out of you today, but I'll get you to talk about it one of these days."

"And I'll talk about it, but not yet. Right now, I just want to pretend the last few months…hell, years of my life never happened."

"No, you don't."

I met her stare, my lips lifting slightly at the corners. "You're right." I sighed. "I don't."

As much as my heart ached from the memory of Dante, he'd shown me how it felt to be free, to be loved, to fly. He gave me my wings. He changed me. Regardless of what the future held, of how much my soul wept without him, I would always be grateful to him for that.

When we reached the crosswalk, I slowed my steps, soaking in the familiar ambience of Los Angeles International Airport. I used to find a sense of comfort whenever I landed back here. The smell in the air. The heat of the sun. The sound of the cars whizzing by as they fought to find curb space to pick up a waiting passenger. Now all these things just made me long for the serenity of rolling green hills, beautiful vines, and warm arms holding me with more love and devotion than I thought possible.

"Feels good to be back home, doesn't it?" Mila remarked, noticing my distant expression. "Or maybe this isn't home anymore."

Biting my lower lip, I stared straight ahead, a heaviness in my limbs. "This is home," I answered, my flat, emotionless voice anything but convincing. "And yes." I faced her, smiling a fabricated smile. "It's good to be back...where I belong."

"Are you sure about that?"

I sucked in a breath, giving her the only answer I could. "I'm not sure about anything right now."

She wrapped an arm around my shoulders, leaning her head against me. "I know. I hate that you're going through this, but we'll figure it all out."

"Thanks, Mila," I offered. "You're a good friend. The only friend I have."

She lifted her head, her expression lightening as a playful smile built on her mouth. "Correction. I'm the only one you *need*. Let's go." She gestured toward the parking garage across the street. "Car's this way."

Once we were situated in her SUV, she drove away from the airport, past several blocks of hotels, finally merging onto the freeway. Red brake lights met us immediately.

"Only in LA," I muttered.

"Why would you want to live anywhere else?" Mila mused, repeating a line I'd said so many times in the past, words I once believed with every ounce of conviction I had. I'd always loved Southern California. The food. The climate. The landscape. The majestic mountains that gave way to miles of pristine ocean. The culture. The diversity. Now it all seemed lacking. It was all different. It was all wrong.

"Why would you?" I mumbled, leaning my head against the window. I felt Mila's eyes on me, studying every move, every facial expression, every breath. Instead of giving her an opening to push more about my time in Italy, I turned to her, my voice bright, masking my pain. I'd spent the last twenty-eight years of my life pretending to be someone I wasn't. This was no different. "So, tell me, anything exciting happen this week?"

"Nothing nearly as exciting as your week."

"Which I don't want to talk about just yet. So make something up to take my mind off everything, okay?" I looked at her with pleading eyes.

She studied me for a protracted moment, then turned her attention back to the road. "Well, Harley decided to say 'Goddammit' over and over again this past weekend."

"There are worse things she could say."

"During church."

I laughed, picturing both Mila's and Steven's horrified reactions. I was certain neither one of them were able to keep from laughing, although I was sure they wanted to.

"Let's see. What else?" She tapped a finger on the steering wheel. "Oh, Ashlyn says she has a new boyfriend. Some little kid we see at the park from time to time. But he's six. Apparently, she has a thing for older men. It's probably a good thing, though. Boys do mature at a slower rate than girls."

"Yes, they do." I settled into the seat, listening to Mila talk about whatever popped into her head. Being the good friend she was, she kept talking, not letting any silence fill the air. Thankfully, she was careful to avoid discussing my failed wedding, Italy, or Dante Luciano.

Finally, after a longer than normal drive, thanks to the notorious LA traffic, she pulled into her driveway in a suburb north of Hollywood.

When I walked into the foyer of her home, I furrowed my brow, the place alarmingly quiet. "Where are the kids?" I expected to be bombarded by a flurry of activity and small voices.

"They're spending the night at their grandma's," she answered, helping me with my bags. "And Steven's working. I figured you could use a little peace and quiet. Plus, we haven't had a girls' night in ages. Probably since your lame excuse for a bachelorette party."

I shot her an annoyed look as I lugged my suitcase up the stairs, heading straight for one of the guest bedrooms.

"What?" she exclaimed. "You only get married once…unless you're Elizabeth Taylor. You're supposed to go big for your symbolic last night of freedom. You're supposed to wake up the next morning, preferably in Vegas, and wonder what the hell happened, not be in bed before ten PM."

"It couldn't be helped," I responded. "Brock and I had a fundraiser to attend the following morning. He would have flipped a gasket if I'd shown up hungover."

"Which is exactly why you should have done it. No woman deserves to be with a man who treats her the way that asshole treated you. I'm just glad you finally opened your eyes and realized that."

I stepped into the small guest bedroom, looking around what was to become my new home for the time being. The only furniture was a bed, a nightstand, and a tiny dresser. I doubted anything else would fit. Approaching the bed, I lowered my laptop bag to the floor with a thump, the weight off my shoulder a welcome reprieve.

"That's all in the past. None of it matters anymore." I faced her as she leaned against the doorjamb.

"I think it still does," she observed thoughtfully. "If it didn't, I don't think you would have gotten on that plane. I think you would have stayed in Rome."

"Mila, that's crazy." I looked everywhere but into her

eyes, not wanting her to see the truth I sought to hide from everyone, including myself. "No one moves their entire world for someone after just—"

She held up her hand, interrupting me. "Not now. Like you said, we have plenty of time to talk later. For now, I'm sure you'd love a shower and a nap."

"My hair definitely feels a bit…greasy." I ran my hand through my dark locks, cringing at the oil that had built up over the past day of travel.

"Do what you need to do. I have piles of laundry to catch up on." She sighed. "The joys of motherhood." She grabbed the knob, about to close the door, but stopped herself. "By the way, I'm glad you fixed that horrendous blonde. You weren't doing yourself any favors with that color."

"Thanks, Mila." I rolled my eyes playfully, then smiled. "It feels good to finally be me again. Whoever that is."

"I think you know exactly who that is, but you're too stubborn to admit it." She paused, allowing her words to sink in, then closed the door, leaving me alone with just my thoughts to keep me company.

Exhaustion setting in, I collapsed onto the bed, relishing in my solitude. Almost instantly, the sound of my phone alerting me to a new text ripped through the silence. A glimmer of hope rushed through me at the idea that maybe Dante had tracked me down and sent a message to tell me he was currently standing outside Mila's front door. Instead, all I saw was a short, curt text from my mother.

Inferno: Part 3
I understand you're back in California after your little "trip". We're hosting a dinner party Friday night, as usual, in case you've forgotten. I expect to see you there. 8 PM.

Groaning, I tossed the phone onto the bed. I had no desire to see my parents anytime soon, or ever, especially with the knowledge my father may have had a role in what happened to Dante's daughter. But a nagging voice in my head reminded me that fate must have wanted me to come home so I could tie up all my loose ends. This was all part of finally stepping out of my parents' shadows. If I didn't face them, if I didn't tell them everything I'd kept at bay for years, I would never be able to close this chapter in my life. So, instead of ignoring my mother, I picked up my cell and shot off a quick text, wishing she could hear the sarcasm in my tone.

Looking forward to it.

With a sigh, I placed my phone back onto the mattress, then stood. Opening my suitcase, I took a sharp breath, completely unprepared to be faced with a physical reminder of my time in Italy. I ran my hand along the silk robe lying on top of all the clothes Dante had bought me. I had almost left everything that would make me think of him and Italy there. In the end, I was able to fit it all in my luggage, with the exception of the gown I wore to the gala, which still hung in Dante's closet in Rome. I wondered what he thought every time he saw it hanging there, if it made his heart ache just as much as mine did at this moment.

Grabbing my toiletry bag, I headed into the Jack and Jill bathroom attached to the bedroom, maneuvering around step stools and toys, and ran the water in the tub, allowing steam to fill the tiny room. I rid myself of my clothes, staring into the mirror. My reflection was devoid of the energy and vitality it had the past week. My lips were pale, the bags under my eyes from the lack of sleep making me appear worn out and beaten down. My skin seemed lifeless. My hazel eyes were dull, dispirited, somber. I no longer looked like the Eleanor I thought I was, the Eleanor Dante brought out. I no longer felt like her, either. I wondered if I ever would again.

Once the temperature of the shower reached the level I preferred, I stepped into the tub, rearranging the curtain so water didn't get all over the floor. I blew out a long breath, allowing the heavy stream to wash off the past twenty-four hours. A thickness formed in my throat at the notion of erasing Dante's touch from my skin.

As I ran a loofah over my body, I closed my eyes and imagined he was with me. His strong, calloused hands exploring every inch of me. His voice murmuring the most salacious and wanton things in that toe-curling Italian accent of his. The fantasy in my head was so real, right down to the tingle running down my spine, reminding me of the last time I had the pleasure of experiencing that high only one man had ever given me.

"Hurry," I begged, tugging at his pants, then practically ripping the buttons off his shirt as I hastily undressed him in the family restroom of the airport. His lips crashed against mine, our teeth clashing against each other, our kiss hungry, desperate, pained. "I need you. Now. One more time."

He lifted me up, slamming my back against the wall as he pushed my panties aside and thrust into me. I released a cry of ecstasy, heartache, and relief, holding onto him as tightly as I could. I feared I'd open my eyes and he'd be gone. I needed to know he was still here, I was still his, that we still had time.

Our breathing became heavy as we nipped and grabbed at each other, taking everything we could with no hint of regret for our greediness. I ran my hands through his hair, my fingers digging into his scalp. I moved against him, urgency and sorrow all wrapped up in one last attempt to hold onto what we had experienced this past week, to have one last moment in the clouds.

My body betraying me sooner than I wanted it to, I threw my head back as fire built inside me, growing hotter until I could no longer control the flames begging to be set ablaze.

"Don't fight it, Eleanor," Dante said, driving into me harder, deeper, fuller.

I shook my head, blinking back my tears. I wanted this moment to last, needed it to last, couldn't come to terms with this ending and having to walk away.

"It's okay. Just let go."

"I don't think I can."

He cupped my cheeks in his hands, peering at me with all the love I never thought I deserved. "Yes, you can. This is the path you've chosen, the path fate has prescribed. It's going to be okay. You'll always have my heart, Eleanor. Always."

"And you'll always have mine," I murmured as I gave in to my desire. My toes curled, my breath catching, my mind blank. Clawing at his back, I tried to erase even the tiniest whisper of distance between us, moaning out his name, my earth shattering around me.

Dante buried his head in my neck, pushing into me with more force, more greed, more agony, then stilled, grunting through his own release. Our bodies remained connected for seconds or hours. At that precise moment, time had no true measurement. We simply held on to each other, neither one of us wanting to break the connection, to return to reality.

When he finally pulled his head away, he looked at me with an expression I couldn't quite label, one that rocked me to my core. He touched his mouth to mine, kissing me in a way he never had before. I felt his body quivering against mine, so I deepened the kiss, holding him tighter. Tears cascaded from my eyes as I tried to take away his heartache, and he mine.

"Ti amo, *Eleanor," he murmured against my lips, his voice wavering.*

"Ti amo, *Dante," I repeated.* "Sempre e per sempre.*"*

"Sempre e per sempre. *No matter what."*

I brushed my thumb against my bottom lip, feeling the ghost of Dante's lingering kiss. "*Sempre e per sempre*," I said through the lump in my throat. "No matter what."

As I slowly returned to the present, I noticed my skin had begun to prune and wondered how long I'd been lost in my fantasy world. I finished showering, then stepped out of the tub and toweled off. After running a brush through my hair, I pulled on one of Dante's t-shirts I'd stolen and crawled under the soft duvet of the double bed in Mila's guest bedroom, wishing that coin had landed on tails instead of heads.

CHAPTER TWO

I SIGHED AGAINST THE fluffy down pillow, pulling the duvet tighter around my body, not wanting to wake up. Dante lived in my dreams now, and I didn't want to leave him, not if this was the only time I could pretend we were still together.

An arm snaked around my midsection and I quickly rolled over, flinging my eyes wide open, trying to make sense of where I was, how Dante was here when I could have sworn I left him. Did he find me already? Or had I snapped under the weight of my broken heart?

Reaching up, I ran my hand along his scruff, delighting in the feel of him, the smell of him, the heat of him. "It was just a dream?"

"What was, *mia cara?*"

I stared into his concerned eyes, not wanting to blink for fear he'd disappear from my bed, my heart, my mind. "Everything," I answered with a tremble, my fingers drifting through his thick, dark hair. "I thought I flipped a coin at the airport in Rome to determine whether I should stay or go. It told me to go. But now…"

He palmed my lower back, bringing me closer. His lips brushed mine, a ghost of a kiss. It wasn't enough. I needed it deeper, needed to feel all of him, to relish in him, to lose myself in him and never come back up for air.

"You did go."

"But—"

He brought his finger up to my mouth, silencing me. "We'll always have our dreams."

"What if that's not good enough?"

He placed a kiss on my nose, wiping my tears. His hands felt rough, just like I remembered. "It'll have to be for now. I promise. I'll always find you there."

"Always?" I asked through my tears.

"Always, my beautiful Eleanor." He drew my head against his broad chest. "Always."

"Always," I murmured, clutching onto him with every ounce of strength I possessed.

When I no longer felt the tickle of his chest hair, I shot upright in bed, staring at the mattress. The only thing beside me was a down pillow.

Running my hand over my face, I took a moment to get my bearings. I was in Mila's guest room. The sun was shining, although I could tell it was beginning its journey toward the horizon. My belongings were strewn all over the little bit of available floor space. And I was alone. No Dante. No arms wrapped around me. No soft murmurs of desire in my ear. Nothing but sadness and emptiness.

I pulled my hair back, securing it in a messy bun, then stood. I was exhausted, but if I kept sleeping, I knew I'd be wide awake in the middle of the night. So, instead of curling up into a ball and pretending my heart wasn't breaking more with each passing second, I trudged down the hallway in search of coffee and my best friend.

"There she is!" Mila's chipper voice called out when I walked into the kitchen. She got up from the couch in the open living room area and headed toward me. "How ya feeling?" Grabbing a mug out of the cabinet, she placed it under her one-cup brewer. The smell of coffee immediately filled the air.

"Better," I answered in a quiet voice, not wanting to tell her about my dream. She eyed me skeptically. "Just recovering from jet-lag, that's all."

"Whatever you say." She turned back around and tore open a packet of sweetener. After adding it, she grabbed the milk from the refrigerator, pouring a bit into the mug, then handed the coffee to me.

"Thanks, Mila."

"Anytime."

I met her forlorn green eyes. Only Mila would be able to know exactly what was going through my mind without me having to say a single word. She knew how I thought, how I processed things. She knew me better than my own parents or the man I was supposed to marry. At that moment, she knew I was barely keeping it together.

"Oh, Ellie." She took the mug out of my hand, setting it on the counter, and wrapped her arms around me. "It hurts like a fucker, doesn't it?"

"More than I thought it would," I choked out, finally

letting my true emotions show instead of keeping them locked away, worried someone would use them to their advantage. Mila would never do that to me. She was the only person who'd ever been real around me, who didn't put on an act. She was who she was, take it or leave it.

"I've been there." She rubbed my back, then pulled away and handed me a box of tissues. Grabbing my coffee, she wrapped her arm around my shoulders, steering me into the living area. "You saw what a wreck I was after our little trip to San Fran all those years ago."

"Yeah, but that's you." I sank onto her comfortable sectional, yanking a stuffed animal out from beneath me and wiping my cheek. "*You've* always been the emotional one." I dabbed my eyes with another tissue, blowing my nose. "This isn't who I am." Tears welled up again and I pulled my legs into my chest, feeling like I was losing control over everything. I'd always been put-together, unaffected, perhaps even a bit cold. In the past few days, I'd shed more tears than I had in all my years combined. "At least it's not who I *used* to be. Now I don't even know who I am, what I'm supposed to do, how I'm going to move on and pretend my life is back to the way it was before all this began."

She placed my coffee on the table in front of us, wrapping me in her arms once more. "You'll figure it out, Ellie. You always do. You don't need to have all the answers right now. Just take this time for you. Relax. Spend hours watching crappy daytime television. Get drunk before noon. You deserve it."

I laughed, drawing in a calming breath as I settled against her chest. "Thanks, Mila."

"You don't have to thank me. This is what friends are for…to be the glue when you're falling apart." She smoothed my hair, just like I did for her in our younger years whenever she came crying to me because of a boy. I never imagined she'd be the one soothing my tears, that she'd be the glue holding me together. "It's big, isn't it?" she asked after several moments of silence, my shaky breaths the only sound filling the room.

I immediately pulled out of her embrace, staring at her with wide eyes. When I saw the devious smile crawl onto her plump lips as she waggled her eyebrows, I burst out laughing. Wiping my cheeks, I grabbed my coffee mug, taking a sip. I'd never been more grateful to have a friend like Mila, a friend who knew exactly what I needed when I needed it. Right now, I just wanted to sit on the couch with her and pretend my world wasn't falling apart around me.

"More than a mouthful," I shot back.

"You hussy!" she joked, playfully punching me in the arm.

I'd never felt comfortable talking about sex before. Now, after Dante opened my eyes, heart, and mind, I didn't feel ashamed about it. It was natural. It was beautiful. It was honest, unlike anything else in my life.

"But I'm glad you finally got to experience real sex."

"Did I ever." I brought my mug back to my mouth, a warmth washing over me as I recalled my week with Dante Luciano. Even when we were fully clothed, there was something so sensual about him. The way he looked at me. The way his presence made me lightheaded. The way his proximity made me ache to touch him, to feel him, to hold onto him and never let go. I'd never met another man like him. I doubted I ever would again.

"What was he like?" Mila asked after a while.

I gazed at the ceiling, considering her question. How could I possibly describe him? Words couldn't do the man justice. The dark eyes that peered into my soul with alarming accuracy. The strong hands that held me captive for days, never wanting to let go. The seductive, raspy tone of his accented voice that I still heard in my head, my brain playing tricks on me, making me think he was beside me when he was thousands of miles away. The impact the absence of all these things had on my heart.

"Powerful. Commanding. Mysterious." I sighed, meeting Mila's eyes. "Beautiful inside and out. After our first meeting, I couldn't stop thinking about him. Granted, when he first spoke to me, I thought he was just some arrogant prick, but I still found myself inexplicably drawn to him. He had this way about him... With just a few words, he'd taken my mind prisoner. After our first kiss, I never wanted to be freed."

"Damn." Mila settled back on the couch, fanning herself. "If you're still this enamored with him, I'm assuming you got some answers about the whole Brock situation."

"I'm sorry," I offered, chewing on my lower lip. "The last few days were a bit of a whirlwind. I meant to call and fill you in…"

She waved me off. "No need to apologize. I was actually glad you didn't call. It meant you worked things out and were getting laid again." She winked. "So what reason did he give for not telling you he was Brock's brother?"

"Because James killed his daughter," I said over the top of my coffee mug before I brought it to my mouth, only to have it ripped away, coffee splashing onto the leather sofa.

"What?!" Mila's eyes looked like they were ready to pop out of their sockets. "Dante Luciano has a daughter?!" She stared at me, stunned, momentarily speechless, which was quite the feat for Mila.

I nodded.

"Holy shit," she breathed. "I'm pretty sure my ovaries just exploded."

I laughed, shaking my head. "I love how I tell you James Harrison may have been responsible for the death of a little girl and the only thing you take away from that is the fact that Dante's a hot dad."

"Hot dad would be putting it mildly. Anyway, that whole family always gave me the creeps. I wouldn't be surprised if they have a secret torture chamber in their basement where they perform experiments on helpless runaways. They're like a walking *Criminal Minds* episode."

"They're not that bad."

"Yes, they are. They're too…perfect. I'd say the same thing about your family if you weren't a part of it. You make your parents normal."

"Only because you made me normal," I reminded her.

"I do my best." She tossed her strawberry-blonde waves over her shoulder. "Now that my ovaries have had time to recover, I need details. Why does he think James killed his daughter?"

"Well…," I began, about to go through the whole sordid tale, but she cut me off.

"Wait a minute. This calls for wine." She jumped up, rushing into the kitchen. She grabbed an open bottle and two glasses off the counter, paused, then grabbed a second bottle. "Lots of wine." She returned to the couch, yanking out the cork with her teeth.

"You've got to stop using your mouth like a kitchen utensil. You're going to lose a tooth one of these days."

"Yeah. Yeah. Whatever." She handed me a glass, pouring the red liquid into it before filling her own.

"Now you may proceed." She sat down beside me as she took a sip. "Dante approached you because he thinks James killed his daughter," she urged. "How did she die?"

"Leukemia," I answered, swallowing hard. "Lilly had leukemia."

She shook her head, covering her heart with her hand. "I couldn't imagine." Then her eyebrows furrowed. "Wait a minute. If Dante had a daughter, why haven't I ever read about her? I certainly would have remembered that little tidbit."

"He wanted it that way. He wasn't married or even in a serious relationship with the girl's mother. The pregnancy was a bit of an accident. But after his own father abandoned him, he didn't want his child to grow up always wondering who her dad was. He didn't want her to be in the spotlight, either."

"He sounds like a good guy, and I'm not just saying that because I want more details about his cock."

"Mila!" I shoved her shoulder. "You're married!"

"I told you! He's my free pass. Steven would want details, too!" She giggled.

"*Anyway*," I continued, my face heating. I proceeded to walk Mila through all the information I'd gleaned from Dante — his daughter's leukemia, her failed intravenous chemotherapy, the doctors putting her on Sprylif, her dying within a week, his reluctance to believe her death was solely due to the disease, the phone call he received from Cynthia Edelman.

"She claimed Lilly's death could have been avoided, that there was a big coverup going on that went all the way up to the head of the FDA."

"Who just so happens to be his biological father, James Harrison."

I slowly nodded.

"Do they have any contact?"

"No. He says James is no more a father than a sperm donor would be."

"What a fuck-tard."

22

I chuckled. "Don't hold back, Mila. Tell me how you really feel." My tone oozed sarcasm.

"What? He is! Especially now that we know he may be corrupt."

"He's not."

"But—"

I opened my mouth, hesitating, unsure how much more I should say.

"What is it? You can't leave me hanging like this. This is better than an episode of *Hawaii Five-0*. We can call it *Italy Six-Nine* since it involves a sexy Italian."

I exhaled, rolling my eyes, then filled her in about the phone conversation I'd overheard between Dante and someone I assumed he'd hired to investigate Lilly's death. "He found emails between her and someone else about the phone calls Dante had made to Barnes looking into Sprylif. The guy on the phone made it sound as if she were ordered to divert Dante's efforts and put the blame on James."

"So James isn't involved?"

"The guy said he had evidence pointing to someone else."

"Who?"

Reluctant, I pulled my bottom lip between my teeth. I had no problem telling Mila that my almost father-in-law may have been responsible for a young girl's death. But the idea that my own father may be the one involved sickened me. I didn't want to say anything until I had more concrete answers. There could have been a completely innocent reason for his contact with Cynthia Edelman, although sneaking around and using an anonymous email certainly didn't make him look innocent.

"He's still working on that," I finally said.

"When do you plan on seeing him again?" Mila asked guardedly.

I released a heavy sigh, pinching my lips together. "We don't have any plans to see each other."

"What?" Mila snapped her head toward me, her eyes wide. "Why not?"

I looked at her, my chin quivering. "Because, Mila. We're too broken. After everything I've been through with my parents and Brock, I need time to learn to be myself. I refuse to be one of those women who becomes so dependent on another person for their own livelihood and happiness that I lose sight of who I am. I just…" I inhaled a shaky breath through the heaviness in my throat, the ache in my chest, the breaking of my heart. I met her eyes, my own brimming with tears. "It killed me to walk away, but I had to. He needs to come to terms with what happened to his daughter, and I need to be on my own for the first time in my life."

Not saying a word, Mila simply reached across the couch, grabbing my hand. That was all I needed. Reassurance from the one person who knew me better than anyone else that I'd made the right decision.

"Do you love him?" she asked.

I stared at her, my silence giving her the answer.

"And you left simply because it wasn't the right

time?"

"I had to," I protested, not sure I wanted to tell her I flipped a coin to decide which path to take, something the old Ellie *never* would have done. "I—"

"Do you know why Steven and my relationship worked, even when I came back home and started college, and we were only able to see each other maybe once a month for four years?"

I shook my head.

"Because we both knew the odds were against us. I was eighteen and he was twenty-two when we met on our girls' weekend in San Francisco. I was starting at San Diego State. He was beginning his last year at Berkeley. I lived in Southern California. He lived up north in San Jose. Nothing about us should have worked, especially when he was across the country at the FBI Academy for six months. But it did because we didn't give up on each other. We both had things to learn. We both needed to discover who we were, what we were meant to be." She wrapped her arms around me and I settled against her. "Sometimes the best love you can find is between two imperfect, broken people who learn to navigate through life's storms together. There are few things worth fighting for, but you can be damn sure love is one of them." She lowered her voice. "Maybe you should have fought more."

"I did," I murmured. "But fate fought even harder."

CHAPTER THREE

WHEN I EMERGED FROM the guest room the following morning after a restless night, vivacious laughter immediately filled the air. I smiled what felt like my first genuine smile since arriving back in LA and headed down the stairs, rounding the corner of the kitchen.

"Auntie Ellie!" two little voices exclaimed the instant they saw me, running from Mila and flinging their tiny arms around my legs.

"Hey, girls." I squatted down, peering into their bright eyes. Both were a mirror copy of their mother, right down to the freckles running across their cheeks and nose. "Did you have fun at your grandmother's yesterday?"

Ashlyn, the four-year-old, nodded enthusiastically. "I got to play outside with her dog." She looked at Mila and Steven standing by the island, drinking coffee. "When can we get a doggie?"

Steven narrowed his eyes as he walked toward her and tousled her strawberry-blonde curls. He looked like he'd just gotten home, still dressed in the dark suit he always wore to the Bureau, although his tie was loosened, the first few buttons of his shirt undone. His sandy hair was a bit disheveled, his blue eyes bloodshot from the obvious lack of sleep. I wondered what kind of case he was currently working on that would have kept him out all night. I had no idea how Mila slept with the thought that, at any minute, her phone may ring with the call all law enforcement spouses must fear. But she never thought too much of it. It was just a way of life for her.

"When your sister's a little bit older." He turned to me as I stood back up, his eyes filled with compassion and worry at the same time. "Hey, Ellie."

"Hey, Steven."

He kissed my cheek, then wrapped his arms around me, giving me a longer than normal hug. I wondered how much Mila had told him. Probably everything. It didn't bother me. They were the only two people who knew the real Ellie...until Dante.

I cleared my throat, cutting through the tension that seemed to be building with each second. "Thanks for letting me crash here."

"You can stay as long as you need. We mean it. A week. A month. A year. Whatever you need until you're back on your feet."

I smiled at him, then shifted my gaze to Mila, giving her a nod of thanks. I doubted I'd be able to get through what faced me on the road ahead without their support. I probably would have had no choice but to go groveling back to my parents or, worse, Brock. I'd never been more grateful to have two friends who would stand by my side, no questions asked.

"I hope I won't need to stay too long." I headed to

the coffee maker and popped a pod in the brewer, then placed a mug underneath. "I came back so I could learn to stand on my own two feet. Living with you guys longer than necessary sort of defeats the purpose. I have some money saved up, but I don't want to eat into that if I don't have to."

"What's going on with your job?" Steven asked.

I shrugged. "No idea. I need to call them today. When I was in Rome, the senior partner left a message. There are only two reasons the senior partner of Sullivan, Sullivan & Grace would call you. I highly doubt it's because he wants to promote me." I rolled my eyes, crossing my arms in front of my chest. "So that only leaves one other explanation." I sighed dejectedly. "But even if he isn't going to fire me, I can't stay at that firm, not when my parents are the only reason they hired me in the first place. I need to get a job based on my qualifications, not because someone owes my family a favor or hopes to get something out of it in return."

"We're here to help, Ellie," Mila offered. "Any way we can. You can use Steven's car for now. He always uses the Bureau's car anyway."

"The only place I really need to go in the next few days is over to Brock's to pack up all my things."

Mila pressed her lips together, her body tensing. "I'll go with you," she said, her voice unwavering, making it known there was no arguing the point. Her eyes floated briefly to Steven, who gave her a quick nod. "We both will."

I never told her exactly what Brock had done in Italy.

28

I didn't have to. She knew. She had tried to warn me about him, tried to tell me something didn't sit right with her. I brushed it off, thinking my parents would never allow me to date someone who wasn't good enough. In retrospect, I couldn't believe how naïve I'd been.

"Thank you." I gave them a sincere look, glancing at the clock on the wall. I released a defeated sigh when I saw the time. "I guess I should call the firm and get this over with."

"I'm sorry." Mila placed her hand on my arm. "I know how much you love what you do."

"It's okay. This is just one more thing I need to cross off my list so I can finally move on with my life." I gave her a reassuring smile, then turned, heading out of the kitchen and up the stairs. Once I was in the guest room, I closed the door behind me and grabbed my cell phone off the nightstand.

A part of me hoped to see a message from Dante, even though I'd refused to give him my number. My heart deflated a bit when the only message was from Brock telling me to come get all my stuff before he sent it to the dump. Someone must have told him I was back. Probably my mother. I'd deal with him later. One issue at a time. That was what I kept telling myself when my brain reeled with everything I had to button up, thinking it would be so easy to apologize, grovel, beg, and go back to my old life. But that wasn't an option. I needed to do this. For me. I'd spent my entire life doing everything for other people, making everyone else happy. Now was the time to focus on myself. And the first step was no longer working at my current law firm.

Unlocking the screen of my phone, I found Mr. Sullivan's contact information, pressed it, then raised my cell to my ear. Almost instantly, his secretary, Paula, picked up.

"Mr. Sullivan's office."

"Hi, Paula. It's Eleanor Crenshaw. I believe Mr. Sullivan is expecting my call."

"Please hold," she said in a curt tone. No small talk. No asking how I was doing. Nothing. I shouldn't have been surprised, but it still caught me off guard that a woman I'd been relatively friendly with in the past would act as if she'd never met me.

After holding for close to five minutes, a voice finally said, "Good morning, Miss Crenshaw."

"Good morning, Mr. Sullivan. I apologize for not getting back to you sooner. I was out of the country."

"Well, I trust that gave you sufficient time to recuperate and reflect after this month's…unexpected events."

I plastered on the expression my mother had spent years coaching me on. Lips curved up slightly at the corners. Eyes interested, but not overly enthusiastic. Chin lifted just a bit. And never, ever let your true emotions show. It didn't matter that he couldn't see me. It was a habit.

"It did. Thank you."

There was a pause on the line, as if he didn't expect

me to be so blasé about what had happened, as if he hoped I'd butter up to him about what a mistake I'd made, what a foolish woman I had been, how I was willing to do anything to make amends. Maybe the old Ellie would have. Not anymore.

"I'm glad you returned my call, Miss Crenshaw," Mr. Sullivan continued, emphasizing his words, as if reminding me that I should have had a different last name at this point. "As I'm sure you can imagine, what happened between you and Congressman Harrison has put you in the public eye. And, consequently, it has put this law firm under scrutiny, as well. We pride ourselves on having associates who are hardworking, honest…and fully committed to our clients. Associates who won't allow personal obligations or issues to affect their work."

My demeanor remained calm as I absorbed what he said. Most people would argue that personal issues should have no bearing on one's professional career, especially someone like myself, who routinely went above and beyond, who regularly worked sixty or eight hours a week, who always got her clients exactly what they wanted. I wasn't going to fight for a job I no longer wanted. Not at this firm anyway. If I had to do some legal aid work or start my own practice, I would. I could help those who really needed it, instead of dealing with mergers, acquisitions, suits between shareholders and parent corporations, and everything else I'd been stuck doing the past two years.

"And since I ran out on my wedding because my fiancé was cheating on me, clients may not feel I'll remain committed to them."

"I'm glad you're so understanding." His voice
brightened. "We've prepared a rather nice settlement
for you, which will be more than sufficient to hold you
over until you're able to secure employment elsewhere,
perhaps a smaller firm."

I briefly closed my eyes, knowing precisely what he
was trying to tell me without saying it. He was going to
make it so I'd never work at a big firm again. I'd
essentially just been sent from the Major Leagues to a
farm team, with no hope of ever returning. I wondered
why he cared so much. Then again, this man went to
law school with my mother and was one of my father's
golfing buddies. If they wanted to make me pay for my
disappearing act from my own wedding, all they had to
do was ask and Mr. Sullivan would certainly comply.
He wasn't going to ruin a long-time friendship with a
powerful senator, even if that senator may be involved
in a child's death.

"I'll have Paula email you the exact details, but we're
offering you full salary for four months. Full health
benefits for a year, unless employment is obtained
sooner. You can keep the company car, and the firm
will be making a substantial contribution to your
401K."

"That is certainly very generous, Mr. Sullivan." I
smiled, my voice exuding all the professionalism I could
muster. It almost seemed like a bribe. He didn't have
any work-related grounds to terminate me. In fact, I
was one of the most promising young attorneys they
had. Yet he wanted me gone, hoping to avoid any

public relation issues that could result from my firing. "But I'm not interested."

"Miss Crenshaw, I—"

"You don't have to buy me off," I interrupted. "I don't want your money. My parents got me this job, and I'm grateful for everything I've learned during my time at your firm. I've had the privilege of working with the very best of the best, but I walked away from my own wedding because I saw my future and didn't like what awaited me. I want to actually work for what I have." I released a small breath, taking a moment to compose my thoughts. "Mr. Sullivan, your father built his business from a one-room office he rented in the back of an accounting firm. He waited by that phone for weeks, hoping a client would call. He *worked*." I shook my head. "I don't know what that's like, but I want to find out. If I take your money, I won't be free from my parents' control, which is what I want, what I *need*."

There was a short pause. I chewed on my bottom lip, unsure how he would perceive my words. Then he finally broke the silence. "Well, you've certainly surprised me, Miss Crenshaw."

I laughed politely. "I'll take that as a compliment."

"It is. You're free to come in and clean out your things when it's convenient. Or I can have them sent to you."

"Don't bother. There's nothing there I need."

"I wish you the best of luck in your future endeavors. I'm sorry this is the way it had to be."

"Don't be. I'm not. Thank you."

"Goodbye, Miss Crenshaw."

"Goodbye." I hung up and sank onto the bed, blowing out a long breath as a weight lifted off my shoulders. I thought I'd be anxiety-ridden with the notion of being officially unemployed and having to find a job in the over-saturated legal market. But after everything I'd been through the past few weeks, I truly believed if it was meant to be, fate would make it so.

CHAPTER FOUR

MILA PULLED THE SUV in back of a rented truck and I glanced to my right at the quaint, two-story cottage in the heart of Brentwood where I lived with Brock the past three years. I didn't know what I expected as I stared at the white exterior and navy blue door. It looked just like it did less than two weeks ago when I hurried down the cobblestone walkway, pulling my luggage behind me, and jumped into this very car so Mila could drive me to the airport instead of First Congregational Church in the heart of Los Angeles where I was to be married. It was as if the past few weeks never happened.

"You don't have to go in if you think it'll be too much." Mila reached over from the driver's seat and squeezed my bicep. "I know what stuff is yours. I'll box it all up."

"No," I sighed. "I need to do this. This is all part of my journey."

Taking a deep breath, I placed my hand on the handle and opened the door, stepping onto the sidewalk. I paused before heading up the walkway, staring at the front of the house. The grass was perfectly manicured. The flowerbeds by the entrance were pristine, not one petal out of place. I helped Brock pick this house out of the dozens of homes he'd looked at. It was on the smaller side, only two thousand square feet, but it had an irresistible charm that was hard to find in the land of cookie-cutter houses and HOAs. At one point in my life, I imagined growing old here. Now it seemed like a foreign place.

I continued up the walkway with Mila as Steven jumped out of the truck and joined us. When I noticed a light snap off in one of the windows on the second floor, I furrowed my brow. Mila must have seen it, too.

"Did you know he would be here?"

I slowly shook my head. "No. When I texted him yesterday, he said he was in D.C. until Friday. That's why I chose to come today."

"Then it's a good thing Steven came with us."

My heart thumped in my chest, my hands growing clammy, my stomach rolling at the thought of facing Brock, of staring into his eyes…eyes that were nearly identical to Dante's. How would I react? Would I break down? Would it make Brock feel like he won?

A part of me wanted to turn around and text Brock to just toss my things so I wouldn't have to see him. I didn't exactly care about my clothes or anything else. But I also knew this was part of cutting the chains tying me to my past. I needed to face Brock again, to let him see he didn't scare me, that I wasn't going to hide from him, regardless of his behavior in Rome.

Squaring my shoulders, I steeled myself. "Let's get this over with." I reached into my purse and grabbed my keys, stepping onto the front stoop. Just as I was about to insert the key into the lock, the door opened.

Brock stood before me, his dark eyes narrowed, a sanctimonious, self-righteous expression on his face.

"Ellie." He crossed his arms over his chest. "So nice to see you again."

"Shut it, Brock." I pushed past him to stand in what used to be my home. Looking around, I realized it had never been a home. I never felt comfortable here. I was never able to just relax on the couch and watch TV or read a book. And God forbid I ever put my feet on the furniture. Brock would call a cleaning crew to have the entire place sterilized.

"I'm trying to be civilized here. I'd appreciate the same courtesy."

I reeled around, my nostrils flaring as I glared at him. I had so many comebacks on the tip of my tongue. I wanted to ask him where his civility was when he decided to break into Dante's apartment and attack me. Where it was when he clamped his teeth on my neck and drew blood. Where it was when he put me in a chokehold and cut off my oxygen. But I didn't. I kept what happened to myself...for now. I had to believe he'd eventually pay.

I clenched and unclenched my fists, then fixed my face into a congenial smile. He wanted to get a rise out of me. I refused to give him that. "I'm just a bit surprised you're here, Brock. We agreed on this date and time because it worked with both our schedules. I was under the impression you would be in Washington."

"A few things came up requiring my attention here. I

was just on my way out. You know… Work. That may seem like a foreign concept to you now that I hear you're unemployed."

As much as I would have loved to smack that arrogant smirk off his face, I just kept smiling. "Do you have nothing else to occupy your time that you still keep tabs on me?" I continued past him and onto the spotless cream carpeting of the living room.

"Ellie!" he exclaimed.

A mischievous grin crossing my mouth, I slowly turned around. I thought he was about to have a coronary based on the expression he wore — his eyes wide, his jaw hard, every muscle in his body tight.

"Your shoes! You know—"

"Oh, how silly of me." I covered my mouth with my hand in a show of feigned remorse. "I forgot the rules." I took my time returning to the entryway, every step on the carpet like another slash of the knife against his skin. I glanced past Brock to see Steven and Mila trying to hold in their laughter. It was a struggle for me, too, but seeing the vein in Brock's neck bulging with irritation and rage made it all worth it.

I slipped my sneakers off my feet, then turned back to Brock. "Don't you have to get going?" I lifted my brows, placing my hands on my hips. "You know… Work."

He glanced nervously between the door and living room, unsure whether he should stay or leave, worried what else I would do to his precious house, what other germs I would bring in.

His lips curling into a snarl, he leaned toward me, his face less than an inch from mine. I flinched. When Steven started forward, I held up my hand, stopping him. I wasn't scared of Brock. He had controlled me for the past ten years. No more.

"If there's so much as a fingerprint on the counters when I get home, you'll regret you ever met me." He pulled back, glaring at me.

"Oh, Brock. I already do." I spun around, heading into the living room and toward the floor-to-ceiling bookshelves, sitting in front of it to start sorting through my books. "Have a nice day at work, sweetie."

I felt his eyes on me for several more seconds, then the front door slammed. I peeked over my shoulder at Steven and Mila, an infectious grin on my face.

"That…was…*awesome*," Mila exclaimed, kicking off her shoes and rushing toward me, dropping to the floor to hug me.

"I don't think I've ever heard you talk to him like that before," Steven commented, carrying the bundles of boxes and packing tape we'd brought with us.

"I haven't. And it felt damn good. Now I can't wait until dinner at my parents' tomorrow night." I began placing some of my books into the box Steven had just assembled.

"I still don't know why you're going over there," Mila sighed, shaking her head.

I stopped what I was doing. "You just saw why. I need to cut the chains they've had shackled around me my entire life. This is how I do it. Not by avoiding them. By facing them head-on. By showing them they can't control me anymore. Trust me."

I returned my attention to the box. I couldn't exactly come out and tell them the real reason I wanted to see my parents. That I needed to find out the truth about my father's supposed involvement in Lilly's death.

"It's going to infuriate my mother when she realizes I'm no longer going to behave like the well-mannered woman she thought she'd raised. That Ellie is gone. This new Eleanor drinks hard liquor. She swears. Hell, maybe she'll even smoke a cigar or two. And she certainly doesn't give a damn about what any of them think of her."

Mila swiftly flung her arms around me again. "God, I'm so glad you got good and fucked by Dante Luciano. He's replaced that stick up your ass with something better."

"Mila!" I admonished, giggling to myself.

"A ginormous cock."

"I can't believe I married you," Steven interjected, laughing.

"You're horrible," I added.

"But you both love me."

I met her eyes. "Yes. Yes, I do."

"Sure do, babe," Steven answered, leaning down to kiss her temple.

We spent the next several hours combing through everything in the house, tossing my things into various boxes — donate, garbage, keep. The stack of boxes containing items I planned to keep was drastically smaller than the others. Most everything here held a memory I wanted to forget. Honestly, there was nothing in this house I couldn't live without, but I needed to be here in order to bid farewell to the last ten years. This was an important step, regardless of how much it seemed like a waste of time.

"I think that's it." I turned to Mila and Steven, placing the last pair of shoes in one of the boxes. Brushing my hands on my jeans, I looked around the master bedroom, not seeing anything else of mine hanging around.

"We'll bring these boxes out to the truck," Mila said. "Do one last check and make sure we got it all. You want to make sure you don't leave any dildos or butt plugs hanging around. Or, better yet, maybe you should. I bet Brock would burn the house down if he saw them."

"Get out of here, Mila." I pushed her into the hallway, her laughter echoing as she followed Steven down the stairs.

I walked toward the reading nook in the corner, which used to be my special little oasis of calm in this house, a place I'd hide to stay away from Brock's critical eyes. I was going to miss sitting in this chair, reading whatever book had my attention that particular day, looking out at the rose garden in the back yard.

I took a minute, my eyes scanning my surroundings. It was a little bittersweet, but in a good way. There was not one ounce of fear, of worry, of trepidation over the idea that I essentially now had no home, no job, no car. I had absolutely nothing to my name, but I didn't need material things to be happy. I had something better. I had love. And, as cheesy and cliché as it sounded, that made me richer than I'd ever been.

Drawing in a satisfied breath, I took one last look, then walked out of the bedroom, closing the door, along with this chapter in my life. As I made my way toward the stairs, I hesitated just outside Brock's office, instantly reminded of his earlier admonition that I not leave so much as a fingerprint on his untarnished counters. A devious grin tugging on my lips, I crossed the threshold and proceeded to his cherrywood desk, not one speck of dust visible on the surface. I sat in his oversized leather chair, spinning around in it. He'd lose his mind if he knew I was in here, which was precisely what I wanted.

Licking my finger, I slid it down the wood, smearing the spotless desk. Then I ran my fingers all over his computer screen, the streaks glaring against the darkness of the monitor. He was going to have a complete meltdown when he came home tonight and sat in this very chair to check the latest stocks, as he did every night. I wished I could be here to see his panic, to see his face turn white with disgust over something as simple as a few fingerprints.

Just as I was about to get up and leave, I furrowed my brow, noticing the top left drawer was slightly ajar. Normally, I would have let it go, but this was Brock. He never left doors or drawers open. Ever. Unless I'd interrupted him when I showed up, which caused him to be careless.

I raised my hand to the drawer, my pulse gradually increasing as I pulled it the rest of the way, revealing a mess of papers. The state of disarray only confirmed my assumption that I must have interrupted him. He never would have left these in such a haphazard state.

Picking them up, I flipped through them, trying to make sense of it all. There was what appeared to be background checks on over a dozen people, along with surveillance photos, some of meetings between one person in particular and my father. It made it look like Brock had been spying on him. Why? Did he know something?

I couldn't make heads or tails of what all these photos and background information could mean. Maybe it was just a coincidence and completely irrelevant to everything I'd learned. But as I neared the end of the pile, I realized this wasn't just a coincidence. Gasping, I dropped the papers when I came across a photo. I'd never seen the woman, but I'd heard the name…Cynthia Edelman. The woman who'd called Dante to try and steer him in a different direction. The woman who'd been corresponding with my father. The woman who had committed suicide on the night she was supposed to meet with Dante.

My eyes raked over her features. Although she was in her early fifties, she didn't look a day over forty. Her lips were full, her gold-speckled eyes large. She had dark hair that contrasted her fair skin. And she had a beautiful smile. I didn't even know this woman, but I couldn't help but feel a sense of loss over her death.

Was this the reason Brock had returned from

Leigh

Washington? Based on all the papers in front of me, he must have figured out something was going on. He had records of Barnes Pharmaceutical employees, including a full background check on Cynthia Edelman. But that wasn't the only pharmaceutical company he had records on. He had reports on various other drugs released from over a dozen companies, from over-the-counter fever reducers to chemotherapy pills, like Sprylif, the drug Dante believed killed his daughter.

My mind spinning, I took my phone out of my back pocket, snapping photos of everything. When I reached the last few papers, my brow furrowed as I stared at two surveillance photos — one of my father walking into Barnes Pharmaceuticals, the other of him leaving. It didn't seem like these were too incriminating. There could certainly have been an innocent explanation. So why would Brock have them?

I spied the time and date stamp on the lower right-hand corner of both — 8:02 PM and 8:25 PM on March 14th of this year. After snapping a photo of the image, I flipped to the next paper, scanning the coroner's report of Cynthia Edelman's death that ruled it a suicide. I looked at the time of death. 8:20 PM. Then I noticed the date — March 14th.

I continued flipping through the rest of the papers, stopping when I came across the police report of Cynthia's death. Apparently, her assistant found her in her office the following morning. She had been so shaken up by the scene that she'd taken a leave of absence. According to her employment record in Brock's possession, she was still on that leave.

With everything I'd learned in Italy and now here, the likelihood that Cynthia Edelman was murdered grew stronger and stronger. It was a bit suspicious that my father had been seen walking into and leaving Barnes Pharmaceuticals on the night Cynthia Edelman, a woman he had sent threatening emails to, took her own life. Something didn't add up here.

"Ellie?" Mila shouted from downstairs. "Are you coming?"

"Just a minute," I called back, grabbing my phone and snapping photos of the autopsy report and the remainder of the papers. Then I put the file back into the drawer, closing it all the way, as Brock normally would have. I didn't know what was going on, but I didn't want him to think I knew anything. There was no telling what he would do with that information.

Chapter Five

I PARKED STEVEN'S CAR in front of my parents' house overlooking the country club in Calabasas, then killed the ignition. There were a few other vehicles parked in the driveway. All of them were luxury, a stark contrast to the economical Ford sedan I currently sat in.

Checking my reflection in the rearview mirror, I reapplied my lip gloss, then tossed it back into my purse. I paused for a moment, staring up at the large two-story stucco house with brick façade that seemed to exude comfort and happiness. But I knew the truth. There was nothing but misery and bitterness residing within those four walls.

Squaring my shoulders, I drew in a calming breath, running my hands over my dress. I shouldn't have been this nervous. This was just like every other Friday night of my life when my mother would host her weekly dinner party, always inviting a different group of people she wanted to impress for whatever reason. Votes. Donations. Or just to fan the flame of her own sense of self-importance. She'd always put on quite the show, and I always went along with it. That all ended tonight.

Brock's indignant look when I finally stood up to him yesterday flashed before my eyes. I laughed slightly. I'd never felt so powerful. I wanted more of that. I had to believe fate had a damn good reason for making that coin land on heads. She knew I needed to be here to tie up all these loose ends, that I needed to show my parents I was no longer going to live under their thumbs.

I stepped out of the car, making my way up the brick walkway toward the front door. My back straight and head held high, I pulled my key out of my purse. Inserting it into the lock, I turned, furrowing my brow when it didn't work.

"Are you kidding me?" I muttered to myself after a few more failed attempts. Even Brock hadn't changed the locks, but my own parents had?

Shoving my keys back into my purse, I rang the doorbell. A chill ran through me when I heard the ominous sound of heels clicking on the marble tile in the entryway. When the door opened, I was faced with my mother's fake smile.

Her unnatural blonde hair was perfectly coifed, falling to just above her shoulders. Despite being over sixty, her skin had the appearance of a much younger woman, thanks to all the Botox injections she'd received in order to fight the natural aging process. Her five-foot, three-inch frame wore a conservative suit, a string of pearls around her neck, channeling her inner Barbara Bush. I'd met the former First Lady. My mother was no Barbara.

"Oh, Ellie," she said in a shrill voice. "There you are. I was wondering if you were going to show at all."

"It's 8:01, Mother. You told me to be here at eight.

I'm not sure being one minute late qualifies for sending out a search party."

"Well, after your little disappearing act at your own wedding, I don't know what to expect out of you anymore."

I bit back the snarky comment begging to spill from my mouth, instead offering her the same exact expression she had on her face — pleasant, cordial, hiding everything.

"Thank you for inviting me."

I walked into the foyer and past the ornate wooden staircase. Most homes had photos of family members, close friends, and loved ones. Not here...unless you counted all the pictures of my father with one important person or another. Diplomats. A few celebrities. And every President since he'd been elected to the U.S. Senate thirty years ago. Not one photo of me.

"If I'd have known you were going to change the locks, I wouldn't have bothered to bring my keys with me," I sneered, getting in one more jab. I had a feeling tonight would be filled with one passive-aggressive comment after another.

"It was simply a precaution, Ellie. For all we knew, you could have been kidnapped by a gang. It wasn't until we saw a photo of you with that...that chef or whoever in Rome that we even knew you were alive." She placed her hand on her heart in a show of feigned compassion. I knew my mother too well to know anything about her was genuine, right down to her lips. "Do you have any idea how concerned we all were?"

She dropped the act, her voice becoming critical, as I was used to. "And why did you change your hair?"

"That *chef*," I began, gritting out a smile, "prefers brunettes." I paused. Noticing her disgust at my response, I decided to go in for the kill. "And spanking...but that's an entirely different conversation."

Incensed, her eyes bulged out of their sockets. "Well, that certainly is *not* appropriate dinner conversation...or any conversation." She grabbed my hand, tugging me toward the formal sitting room where I was certain my parents' stuck-up friends would be lounging while Maria, our housekeeper, finished preparing dinner. "Please remember your place tonight. We'll discuss your recent behavior later, but tonight, we need to give off the impression that you're normal."

"I *am* normal, Mother. It's you and Dad and everyone you surround yourselves with who are anything but normal and genuine. I'm done with it all."

"Not now, Ellie," she hissed.

"Of course not. We wouldn't want someone to think you're anyone other than the gracious wife of a senator, would we? We wouldn't want anyone to realize you're a miserable, self-centered, egotistical shrew who gets off on everyone else's failings." I smiled, then abruptly turned from her shocked expression and continued into the sitting room where four older couples sat. The men drank scotch, while the women held glasses of champagne or club soda. It was such a double-standard and I despised it. Just because we were born with ovaries instead of testicles we couldn't handle the hard stuff?

"There's my little Houdini!" my father's jovial voice bellowed the instant I crossed the threshold. I immediately stilled as I stared into his brilliant blue eyes, his smile seemingly kind. Like my mother, he masked everything under his bright expression and charming demeanor.

I swallowed hard, doing my best to act as if I didn't know about the secret he was hiding, how dark his heart truly was, how cruel he must be to be involved in something to cause harm to another human, particularly a child. I wanted to rip into him, especially in front of this small gathering, but I kept my mouth shut. I needed to approach this carefully, to slowly let out just a little bit of rope at a time, ask a few seemingly innocuous questions, each one tightening the noose until he hung himself. I'd been around politicians my entire life. I knew how they played their game. And I planned on beating him at it.

"Very funny, Dad." I laughed with a fabricated smile.

"We were very worried about you," he said, not getting up from his position on one of the divans. "Something horrible could have happened to you."

Everyone else nodded in agreement, a forced expression of concern etched on each of their faces. I glanced around the room, taking inventory of the people my mother had invited to the weekly show, as I liked to call it. First, we had the neighbors, Richard and Jackie Bennigan, who must have been in town on a stopover to wherever they were heading next. They didn't spend much time in California, and the house next door wasn't their primary residence. Richard was the CEO of one of the banks still standing after the financial crisis a few years ago. I found it odd that he purchased a brand new yacht and villa in Aspen just days after his bank received the bailout money. Politics at its finest.

Then there were Liam and Gretchen Young. He was a neurosurgeon and she was a homemaker, although their household staff did most of that. She came from old money and devoted her free time to various charities, or so she said. Just like everyone else I'd been surrounded with, I doubted she did much more for these charities than write a check.

Next was Lucas Merriweather and his current flavor of the month, who couldn't have been more than a few years out of grad school. The older Lucas got, the more juvenile his taste in women. He was one of the most sought-after advisors and strategists in politics today, not to mention the man who'd run every single one of my father's campaigns. He wouldn't be anywhere without Merriweather's expertise, and my father knew this. Worse, so did Lucas. After all, he'd learned from the best. His father was a force to be reckoned with in politics, as well, having advised my grandfather and great-grandfather. Lucas simply carried on the family legacy. His influence had become so pervasive it was sometimes difficult to remember who the elected official truly was.

Last was Edward and Freida Sullivan...the same Mr.

Edward Sullivan who fired me just a few days ago. Of course, he acted as if everything were the same, as if nothing had changed. But I'd changed. And I couldn't be more grateful for the lightbulb finally going off. For having the guts to stand up for myself. For Dante.

I studied the females in the room, each of them sipping their drinks. They all looked bitter, like they hadn't had a real orgasm in years…or ever. Like they'd never been loved. Like they'd never been swept off their feet by a man who pledged to cherish them until their dying day. I no longer resented these women for perpetuating the cycle, for refusing to take advantage of the advances our gender had made over the years, to embrace their sexuality. Instead, I pitied them for how sheltered they were, how unloved they were, how miserable they were. Yes, they had more money than they could ever spend in a lifetime, but that couldn't make up for what they'd missed out on… Passion. Excitement. Unrivaled joy. I'd rather die penniless with no possessions than be stuck in a life of lies, façades, and emptiness.

"Pleasure to see all of you." I smiled, ignoring my father's comment, then walked toward the wet bar, surveying the choices. I typically drank champagne, as was expected of me, but I was no longer going to do that. Grabbing the bottle of scotch, I poured a few fingers into a tumbler before rejoining my parents' guests.

"There's champagne, Ellie," my mother said through clenched teeth, laughing politely. I hadn't noticed her follow me into the room once her shock had worn off.

"Some wine, as well."

"I'm aware. I'd prefer a glass of scotch right now." I sat and leaned against the back of the upright chair, shunning all the etiquette classes I'd been forced to endure throughout my life. Hell, if I really wanted to give my mother a heart attack, I'd scratch my crotch, but that may have been taking it a bit too far.

She stared at me, her lips formed into a tight line, telling me without words that she didn't approve of my actions. I didn't care. I no longer craved her approval. When she realized I wasn't going to behave as she wanted, she tore her eyes from mine, smiling cordially at all her supposed "friends", although I was certain she didn't truly appreciate what being a friend entailed. It meant giving unwavering support. It meant loving them unconditionally. It meant sacrificing your own needs for them. It certainly didn't mean looking down your nose when they did something you didn't approve of, then speaking poorly of them the instant they were out of earshot. My mother could have all the manners and etiquette classes in the world, but she failed to learn how to be a decent human being. It was a wonder I turned out as normal as I had.

"I understand you saw Brock yesterday," she began, all eyes in the room shifting to her, feigning interest in the conversation.

"I did. I went to his house to box up all my things."

She furrowed her brow. "Box up your things? Why would you do that?"

"Because we're not together anymore." I took a sip of

the scotch, trying to hide my grimace. I didn't particularly care for the stuff, but I refused to give in to my mother's expectations.

"That's because you won't hear him out. He was very upset when you stood him up...at his own wedding!"

"He deserved it," I shot back. "In fact, he deserved worse after I walked in on him *banging* his secretary."

Mrs. Young let out a slight gasp of disapproval and nervously looked around the room, which had grown thick with tension. "I believe I may have found the perfect entertainment for the annual charity art show," she said, obviously trying to change the subject to one not so displeasing to her supposed delicate sensibilities, as if the idea of sex was too obscene. It made me laugh inwardly at the ridiculousness of the life I used to live.

"Perhaps he wouldn't feel the need to stray if you were able to...satisfy him," my mother retorted.

I blinked repeatedly, unable to believe this woman gave birth to me. You'd think a mother would console her daughter after she'd ended a ten-year relationship because her fiancé had been unfaithful. Not my mother. This was just another way for her to find something lacking with me, another example of how I was a failure as a human, another instance where I'd fallen short of her ridiculous expectations.

"He tracked me down in Rome. Did you know that?" I glowered at her, my lips in a tight line. I'd tried my best to stay collected and even-tempered, not wanting her to see she was getting to me, but it grew more and more difficult the longer I spent time here, disgust filling me as I was faced with the reminders of how weak I'd been for years.

"That's very romantic," Jackie Bennigan said, everyone in the room nodding in agreement, except my father, which struck me as odd. Unease flickered in his gaze, as if he knew there wasn't a good reason for Brock to fly halfway around the world to find me when I'd made it perfectly clear I didn't want to be found. Then again, it could have been an act, just like everything else.

"Oh, it was," I replied, my voice heavy with sarcasm. "I'm not sure which part was more romantic." I looked up at the ceiling, as if deep in thought. "Him breaking into where I was staying. Him pinning me to the ground and biting my neck, drawing blood." I returned my eyes to the room, stunned expressions surrounding me. "No. That's not it."

My gaze turned cold. I didn't know what had come over me. I never even told Mila exactly what happened when Brock found me. I didn't have to. She saw past the golden boy persona and knew what he was really like, something I'd been too blind to see for years. No longer. And these people needed to see it, too.

"The most romantic part was probably when he forced me to the floor, covered my body with his so I couldn't get up, then wrapped his arm around my neck, cutting off my oxygen, and threatened to kill me."

I glanced around the room, a mixture of stunned, confused, and uncomfortable expressions staring back, except for my mother's.

"Oh, Ellie." She waved her hand, downplaying what I'd just admitted. "I'm sure it wasn't like that or he would have been arrested. As always, you're blowing things out of proportion."

With an unfocused gaze, I cocked my head at her, my mouth becoming slack. "Out of proportion?" I repeated, my body tensing as I gripped my glass tighter.

"You were probably just a bit emotional over everything. Brock would never do anything to harm you. That's preposterous. Were you drinking at the time?" she sneered, eyeing the tumbler in my hands.

"You're unbelievable," I murmured, then stood, gritting a smile at my parents' guests. "If you'll excuse me for a minute." With determined strides, I stormed out of the room and down the hall, yanking open the sliding glass door leading to the back yard.

Once I emerged onto the patio, I downed my drink, needing the burn of the liquor to soothe my anger. I didn't know why I expected my mother to react any differently. I never thought she'd wrap her arms around me and ask if I was okay, but I hoped she'd at least believe me. To think she was so delusional and uncaring as to accuse me of exaggerating about what happened boggled my mind.

Slamming the empty glass onto a nearby lounge table, I formed my hands into fists, smothering back a scream. That was precisely the response my mother wanted. She wanted me to have a meltdown in front of her guests. She got a rise out of it, thinking it made her appear superior. I wouldn't give that to her. I couldn't let her see that she got to me.

My nostrils flared, my teeth grinding as I paced back and forth by the pool, trying to settle my anger and distaste. I came to a stop by the railing at the edge of their property high on the hill and leaned my arms on it, taking in the view. I used to love sitting out here and looking at the lights twinkling below me in the valley, the mountains in the distance. Now my surroundings only made me long for the rolling hills of Dante's vineyard in Italy.

I closed my eyes, wishing I were still there, that Dante would find me at any moment and wrap his arms around me, whispering words of love in my ear. The image of him soothed the fire raging inside, calming me. I'd never felt so unbalanced in my life. I believed getting on that plane and coming home was the right thing to do. Now I thought everything would have been better had I stayed.

"Looks like you could use this," a voice said. Snapping my eyes open, I looked to my left to see my father holding out a glass filled with quite a hefty pour of scotch toward me, surprising me.

"Dad, what are you—"

"Can't I have a minute alone with my little girl? Maybe have a drink together?"

My brows gathering together, I hesitantly took the glass, raising it to my lips as he brought his own drink to his mouth. I sipped it, the burn not as strong as the one I'd poured for myself earlier.

"I added a bit of water to it," he explained. "You can

still piss your mother off by drinking it, but at least it won't sting as much."

I nodded, remaining silent as I returned my eyes to the houses dotting the sprawling metropolis. The air was thick with an awkward tension, neither one of us saying anything. There was a time I used to be comfortable around my father, especially when it was just us and he could drop his public persona. When he would simply be my dad, not the man who defied the odds and won the open Senate seat as a Republican in a state that typically leaned blue. The dad who took me horseback riding, and not side-saddle, as my mother requested. The dad who let me trade in my figure skates for a pair of hockey skates. The dad who brought home a dog for me…until my mother made him get rid of it. I still had trouble reconciling that man with the man he had become in recent years, the man who could be responsible for a little girl's death, and perhaps more that I didn't know about.

"What you said in there…," he began after a few moments.

I turned to look at him, his blue eyes weary, the creases around his face exhibiting his age. My father always had a sort of youthful exuberance about him, even as he neared the age of seventy. But despite the silver hair and growing number of wrinkles, he was still handsome, his tall stature and broad chest making him look like the powerful politician he was.

"Was it… Did he…?" His lower lip trembled, surprising me.

Once I'd entered adolescence, my father and I seemed to grow apart. In my eyes, he became just as obnoxious and uncaring as my mother. Now, as I saw the emotion and something resembling fear covering his face as he stared at me with guilt in his eyes, I caught a glimpse of the man I remembered him to be during my younger years. Maybe this was all part of his act. This man...this family...made me so jaded. I had no option but to take any show of compassion with a grain of salt, to wonder what game he was playing by being so caring.

"He did."

He released a quivering breath, closing his eyes, his shoulders slumping forward. "Ellie, I..." Running a hand over his face, he peered at me, at a loss for words. "Why wasn't he arrested? How did you—"

"A man found me when I needed him most." A nostalgic smile crossed my face, a warmth spreading through me as I considered how those words were true in more ways than one.

"Dante Luciano?" My dad lifted a brow.

"Yes. He came just at the right time."

"But why wasn't Brock arrested? If he hurt you..."

"Because." I held my head high, needing to get this off my chest. I faulted him and everyone else for never being real or genuine. So he needed to hear something he may not be used to...the truth. "When I walked in on Brock and his secretary, something inside me snapped. I looked at my life, at the people in it. I saw myself turning into Mom if I continued on the path I'd been on, and the thought sickened me. I went to Italy to find myself, to give myself a fresh start. If I had Brock arrested, I'd be thrown back into the life I ran from." I waved my hand around. "This life. I'm done with it. I'm done being a pawn in Brock's game, in Mom's game....in your game."

I expected him to argue that he wasn't playing any game. Instead, a look of understanding came over his face. "It wasn't always like this," he said after a pause.

"What?" I pushed.

"Everything. We were in love once, your mother and I. At least, I thought we were."

"What happened?" I asked, taking a sip of my scotch and water.

"I guess love and happiness stopped being important. Image, power, and winning took a front seat to everything else. And I let it. Soon, I was trapped with no way out." He turned his eyes from mine, looking over the valley. "Don't let that happen to you."

All I could do was nod. I'd probably spoken more to this man in the past five minutes than I had in the last ten years. A part of me was filled with sympathy when I noticed the longing on his face, as if he were remembering happier times, but I didn't allow it to sway me. He'd fooled the American people into thinking he was some beacon of morality, that he would clean up corruption in Washington. I knew the truth, though. He was just as corrupt as the rest of them.

Finally, after a long silence, I asked the question that had been on the tip of my tongue all night. "Have you ever had any dealings with Barnes Pharmaceuticals?"

His eyes immediately shot to mine, wide, worried...afraid. "What did you say?" Then understanding fell over him and he nodded. "Dante Luciano..."

I didn't agree or disagree, not wanting to give too much away.

"Brock told you they're half-brothers, didn't he?"

My expression remained unwavering as I let out a little bit more rope, wondering how much more he needed to hang himself.

"This whole thing is a ticking time bomb." He ran his hands through his hair, tugging at it.

"What is?" I pushed, my heart thumping in my chest.

"I don't even know. All I *do* know is something's going on. People have lost their lives when they've gotten too close to figuring out what that is. You need to walk away."

"Walk away?"

"Don't ask questions, Ellie. Please," he implored, his tone borderline demanding. Then he leaned closer, his voice no louder than a whisper. "Stay away from this. I may not have been able to protect Dante's daughter and dozens of other people, but I *can* protect you."

I pulled back. The fear I saw, the pleading, the anxiety, the panic... I wanted to believe it was real. I wanted to believe he was worried for my well-being, that he'd do anything to protect me. But I had twenty-eight years' worth of reasons I couldn't. He could put on an act for the public, make them think he was this upstanding politician, but I knew what he was like.

It was only a matter of time until the rest of the country realized it, too.

CHAPTER SIX

"WHERE ARE YOU OFF to?" Mila asked when I walked into the kitchen Monday morning dressed in a dark gray suit. "Do you have an interview?"

"No," I answered, doing my best not to let her see how discouraged I was as I grabbed a travel mug and brewed a cup of coffee. I'd spent the majority of my time since returning from Italy scouring the internet for any job in the legal field I was even remotely qualified for. There were plenty of openings, but none paid close to what I had made at my old firm. I couldn't let that deter me, though. I needed to start somewhere, even if that meant having to struggle for a little while.

"Then where are you going dressed all business-like?"

I finished fixing my coffee the way I took it, then faced her as she made some oatmeal for the girls. "I'm not sure yet. I have a list of lawyers who were opposing counsel on the cases I previously worked on. Maybe if I run into them, get a little face time, I may be able to talk my way into a job."

"So you're just going to drop in at all these firms?" She lifted a brow as she stirred the oatmeal.

"No." A conniving smile crossed my mouth. "But I know where they like to grab their coffee when they need their mid-morning break." My expression fell and I shrugged when I saw the skepticism on Mila's face. "It's worth a shot. Better than sitting here and hoping my phone rings with someone wanting to schedule an interview."

Mila stopped what she was doing and placed her hands on my shoulders, giving me an encouraging smile. "You're a brilliant woman, Ellie. They'd be crazy not to hire you. Just like your old firm was crazy to let you walk away from them."

"Thanks, Mila."

Her confidence in me was exactly what I needed at that moment. I'd never sought out anyone's assurances. I always had tenacity in spades. But that was before. With each day that my phone didn't ring with a potential job, my determination and belief in my abilities began to waver, even though I'd only been back a week. I guess I didn't think it would be this difficult, particularly with the credentials I brought to the table.

"You bet. Have a good day lawyer stalking," she called out as I headed from the kitchen.

I stopped to give Ashlyn and Harley a kiss goodbye on my way out the door, then hopped into Steven's car to begin the traffic-filled journey toward the Starbucks by the courthouse in downtown LA.

I sat in that coffee shop all day, updating my resumé, searching for jobs online, trying not to think about my father and his situation as I waited for a familiar face to pop in. And many did. We would chat about the unseasonably high temperatures, the drought, how long it took to get hearing dates set by the court clerk. Everyone seemed a bit antsy around me, not wanting to bring up the wedding that never was and the job I no longer had. Whenever I broached the topic of whether their firm may be hiring, they were suddenly late for a meeting. I shouldn't have been surprised, but it still stung to think that the one thing I loved, the one thing I was good at, had been ripped away from me, too.

Day after day, I chatted with some of my colleagues in the legal profession. And day after day, they rushed off the instant I mentioned any job openings. After a week of nothing but rejection, I stopped dressing in a suit, opting for a comfortable sundress or pair of capris instead. I branched away from the courthouse area, deciding to take advantage of my unemployment to explore LA. I found some beautiful parks hidden away and would sometimes sit beneath the shade of a tree and people-watch. Occasionally, I thought I saw Dante sitting in the same park, or riding in a passing bus, or walking on the opposite side of the street, but reminded myself it couldn't be him…and it never was.

The more time that went on, the more frustrated I became about my current situation, the more I saw him everywhere. He was the barista at Starbucks. He was the hipster playing Frisbee in the park. He was the tortured artist sketching while he waited for the train. With nothing but my thoughts to fill my time, I found myself missing him more and more, the pain like a vice squeezing my heart.

To keep from completely breaking down at the

morose direction my life had taken as of late, I started playing a game. No matter where I was, what I was doing, where I was going, I pretended Dante was just around the corner, that he was on his way to meet me, that I was mere seconds away from being in his arms again. It was the only thing that kept my idle mind from wandering, from thinking about what he was doing, from wondering whether I'd imagined the whole thing.

So I allowed myself to remain hopeful, thinking when I crossed the street, entered a shop, sat in the park, he would be there. He never was, but keeping the hope alive was all I had, regardless of how misplaced that hope was. I drew comfort in the fact that I could look at the same sky, fall asleep beneath the same moon, and wish on the same stars, praying this would all work itself out.

This hope, this faith, this dream was the only thing that kept me from having a complete meltdown as I lay awake in Mila's guest room each night, the double bed I slept in cold, wondering whether I'd made the biggest mistake of my life by getting on that plane and coming back to the States.

I had no job. No home. No car. No family. I couldn't lose my hope, too. Hope was all I had left.

~~~~~~~~~~

ON A THURSDAY IN July, as I was leaving MacArthur Park in Westlake, fate finally intervened, albeit in a small way. I'd been back for a month, but was still jobless, homeless, carless, and becoming closer and closer to being penniless with each passing day. When I attended my mother's weekly Friday evening dinner parties, my father offered to loan me some money, which I vehemently refused. That would defeat the purpose of my returning here, not to mention he could have been trying to buy my silence in regards to whatever he was involved in. I kept trying to get him to talk about what he knew, but he remained silent. There was only so long someone could remain tightlipped, and I hoped to be there when the dam finally broke.

As I was about to cross the street to begin the drive back to Mila's, I came to a quick stop when a metro bus nearly hit me, despite the fact I had a WALK signal. It took me a minute to recover. When I did, my shock only heightened as I came face to face with an image of Dante on the side of the bus in an advertisement for the upcoming season of his show.

I remained frozen in place, my mouth agape, blinking repeatedly, no longer startled that I'd almost been hit by the bus. My gaze was glued to Dante's smiling face, his perfect white teeth, his arms crossed in front of his chest, his biceps stretching the fabric of his shirt. It was one thing to live in my fantasy world where I pretended I would see him whenever I turned a corner or crossed a street. It was another to stare at a life-sized image of him. I'd done my best to stay strong, to tell myself this was all part of fate's plan. Now I felt like fate was a cruel, sadistic bitch taunting me, reminding me of everything I once had but threw away.

The driver of the bus looked at me with apologetic

eyes, then gestured for me to cross. I shook my head, stepping back onto the sidewalk, waving him on. I doubted I could put one foot in front of the other at that moment, my legs weak, my hands shaky.

For weeks, I'd seen Dante everywhere, heard him everywhere, *felt* him everywhere. But I knew those people weren't really him. This was different. I'd done my best to steer clear of all reminders of him. I refused to watch TV and avoided all social media on the off-chance I may catch an unexpected glimpse of him. His face had slowly faded from my memory, the curves, dimples, and perpetual five o'clock shadow gradually becoming little more than a dream. And I'd begun to wonder if I *had* dreamt it all.

Now that I was faced with a reminder of the man I'd spent a week with, I knew I hadn't. I remembered that cocky smile, his teeth flashing from across the aisle of the airplane. I remembered the brush of his fingers on my shoulders as he hung his jacket on me to keep me warm. I remembered the feel of his breath on my skin, every muscle in his body becoming tight as he moaned my name. He was real. What we had was real. The ache in my heart was real.

Once the bus continued past me and disappeared out of sight, I took a moment to pull myself together, then hurried across the street and jumped into Steven's car. I spent hours driving aimlessly around LA, doing everything to get the image of Dante's mysterious eyes, breathtaking smile, and full lips out of my mind. Trying to forget how perfect it felt when he wrapped his strong arms around me, swallowing me whole. Trying to forget the love we shared for a too-brief moment in time. I hated it. Hated this feeling. Hated Dante for making me feel this way, for shattering the walls I'd built around my heart, for showing me how it felt to fly.

As I drove, I swore I saw him everywhere, more so than usual. I even called out a few times to complete strangers who I thought looked exactly like him, only for me to realize there was no resemblance at all, my brain playing a cruel trick on me. After the fourth such encounter, I pulled off the road, thinking I shouldn't be operating a vehicle in my current state.

I tugged on my hair, my heart rate picking up, my breathing increasing. Gripping the steering wheel, I fought back a scream as the world around me spun out of control. This was it. I'd lost my mind. I was jobless, homeless, penniless. It was only a matter of time until I became a crazed woman begging beneath the bridges downtown. All it took was seeing Dante's face to make me lose control of everything I'd kept at bay since returning home.

"Where did I go wrong?" I asked myself softly as I stared out the window at the setting sun, a slight breeze blowing the tree branches.

When I came back from Italy, I had a vision for what my life would be like. I would quit my job and get a new one. I would tell my parents I was done with them. I would find my own apartment and buy my own car. It had been a month, but my life wasn't even close to resembling any of that. All I'd done was quit my job. I'd yet to find a new one. I still saw my parents once a week. I was living in my best friend's guest room, which was smaller than Dante's walk-in closet, and driving her husband's car. It was a miracle I'd been strong enough to not go crawling back to Brock. I hadn't seen him since the day I boxed up my things. That was the only silver lining in my life, the only thing that had gone right, although I was just waiting for the bottom to drop on that, too.

Drawing in deep breath after deep breath, my muscles eventually began to relax, my tears slowly subsiding. When I felt relatively calm again, I started the car and navigated back toward the freeway. I took my time as I drove north to Mila's house in the suburbs, stopping for dinner and a strong drink along the way. I was in no rush to walk into her perfect family dinner, to be faced with a reminder of everything she had that I didn't. I loved my friend. I loved that she found someone who made her happy. I loved how much she supported me during this trying time in my life. But everything hurt a little too much today. Maybe tomorrow would be better, but right now, I just needed to be alone with my heartache.

It was dark when I finally pulled into Mila's driveway. Killing the engine, I looked up at the house, a peaceful tranquility about it, at complete odds with the turmoil and storm raging inside me. The last few hours a complete blur, I eyed the time to see it was after ten. The girls would be asleep, and I assumed Mila would be getting ready for bed herself. Not wanting to disturb anyone, I did my best to make as little noise as possible as I unlocked the door and headed through the darkened living room and toward the stairs. When I was safely enclosed in the guest room, I let out a long breath.

I kicked off my shoes and stripped out of my clothes, throwing on Dante's old t-shirt, his scent having faded over the weeks. After brushing my teeth, I slipped into bed and pulled the duvet tightly around me, pretending it was Dante's arms keeping me warm. I tossed and turned for hours, sleep evading me.

Close to midnight, my phone buzzed with an incoming text. My heart jumped, a misplaced hope building in me that it was Dante, that he could sense my struggle, but I knew it wouldn't be. Instead, the text was from Mila.

> *I'm up if you want to talk.*

I didn't know how she could tell I had a rough day. As much as I appreciated the offer, I just couldn't. Not right now. I just wanted to wallow, to cry, to hurt. Then maybe I could finally start healing. I could finally start the next chapter in my life. I could finally let go. Maybe this was fate's way of telling me I *needed* to let go, to move on.

> *Thanks. I just want to sleep. We'll talk tomorrow.*

She replied almost instantly.

> *Okay. Love you.*

I was about to click the screen off when my eyes fell

on the Facebook icon in the lower right corner, almost mocking me, begging me to press it. I didn't know what came over me at that moment. Maybe it was the combination of feeling like a failure and seeing Dante's beautiful face earlier that pushed me forward when I normally would have warned myself that what was meant to be would be. The truth was, I missed him. And I wanted to surround myself with a reminder of him, even if it came in the form of stalking his Facebook page. Even if it ripped my heart to shreds.

Despite my brain telling me to just fall asleep, I entered Dante's name in the search bar and navigated to his official page. It was mostly information about shows currently airing and possible locations for the next season of his series. I could tell it was probably run by his staff. This was the Dante Luciano everyone else knew. It wasn't the Dante Luciano *I* knew. I wanted to see *that* Dante. The Dante who made love to me in his vineyard. The Dante who kissed me in front of the Trevi Fountain like no one was watching. The Dante who begged me to consider a future with him.

I almost put my phone back on the nightstand, but decided to look at his Instagram account first. I'd watched his show in the past, recalling him snapping photos routinely during the episodes that aired. Those photos must be posted somewhere.

I opened the app, typed his name in the search bar, then clicked on his official Instagram page, scrolling through thumbnails of hundreds upon hundreds of photos from his travels, some of them selfies. I could instantly tell that Dante had put his mark on each and every photo posted. This was what I wanted. Not some page promoting shows and appearances.

Scanning the photos, I marveled at the images. This man had been everywhere. I doubted there was a country he hadn't visited, apart from North Korea and the Arctic. Even then, if he could find a way to go, he probably wouldn't hesitate. He was in some of the photos, others were just incredible shots of his surroundings. Many didn't require any sort of filter, showing how truly remarkable this planet was. There were some places I'd never seen before. Others were from more noticeable locales — the Eiffel Tower, the Great Wall of China, the Pyramids.

As I continued scrolling through the feed, my breath caught when I noticed a shot of a place that was all-too-familiar. I clicked on the thumbnail, bringing up a larger version of it, and swallowed hard as I stared at a wide shot of the Spanish Steps. It must have been taken from the top, the plaza and fountain perfectly visible from his perch. To the far right was the tea room he'd taken me. To the far left, I was able to make out the narrow street leading to his apartment. I could almost hear the busy chatter from all the tourists. I could almost smell the scent of the city. I could almost feel Dante standing beside me.

Then I noticed something. If I hadn't been there and remembered precisely where I stood when Dante had approached me that day, I never would have seen it. But there I was...directly in the center of the photo, pacing in front of the fountain, wondering whether I could really go through with what I'd intended to simply be a one-night stand.

My eyes floated to the caption.

> *"I'll say she looks as clear as morning roses newly washed with dew."* - *William Shakespeare, The Taming of the Shrew.*

I brought my hand to my mouth to cover my trembling chin. This photo was further evidence of his claim that when we finally slept together, it wasn't to get information. It was because he was drawn to me, just as I was to him. It made my soul ache with regret. I wondered if I would have taken a different path had I seen this before getting on that plane.

Backing out of the photo, I scrolled through everything he'd posted during my week in the clouds, clicking on every single one. To the casual observer, they simply appeared to be travel photos, some staged. But I knew better. This was Dante's love letter to me.

I couldn't help but sigh contentedly when I stopped on a photo of his breathtaking bedroom in his villa in Tuscany where we'd spent the second half of my week in Italy. The French doors were open, the sheer curtains blowing in front of them. The sun streaked long lines against the hardwood floor. I could almost picture myself in that room at this very moment. I focused just past the curtains, able to make out my silhouette as I leaned against the railing, gazing out over his expansive vineyard.

Then I read the caption of this one.

Inferno: Part 3
"I burn. I pine. I perish." - William
Shakespeare, The Taming of the Shrew.

"Oh, Dante," I exhaled, swiping at the tears steadily falling down my cheeks. But they were no longer tears of sorrow. They were tears of pure joy, of ecstasy, of love. Pain no longer filled me, regret no longer ate me up. I found exactly what I needed...affirmation that our love was real, that it was true, that it could transcend the ocean, the miles, the distance. That it would all work out.

I continued scrolling through several dozen more photos that were obviously meant for me, many containing various quotes from one of Shakespeare's plays or sonnets. I stopped when my eyes fell on one that was taken on my final day in Italy. The photo showed two hands on a pillow. The room was dark, apart from a bit of a glow from the moon. Just beyond our linked hands was my face, my eyes closed, a lone tear falling down my cheek. I thought I had stayed up all night with Dante, but I must have dozed off at some point, giving him the chance to snap this beautiful, heartbreaking photo. My eyes floated to the caption.

"For where thou art, there is the world itself.
And where thou art not, desolation." - William
Shakespeare, Henry VI.

Blinking back my tears, I allowed the words and image to bathe me with the love and pain Dante must be feeling at this moment, as well. Until this evening, I thought I was alone. In my despair. In my regret. In my grief. The knowledge I wasn't reinvigorated me with the same hope that had pushed me forward each day since our separation began.

Feeling inspired, I turned on the lamp, allowing a subtle glow to fall over the bed. I did my best to recreate the same pose from the photo, minus one very important hand. When I thought I had it just right, I added a filter to make it a bit darker, then Googled for an appropriate quote, finally finding one.

> *"Who could refrain that had a heart to love and in that heart courage to make love known?"* - *William Shakespeare, Macbeth.*

I added a few hashtags and was about to post the photo when my eyes fell on the option to tag someone. Maybe it was the lack of sleep. Maybe it was the loneliness. Maybe it was the need to experience Dante's love. As much as I tried to put my faith in fate that we'd find our way back to each other, I missed this man. More than the skies missed the stars. More than the plants missed the sunlight. More than the dawn missed the day. In my moment of sorrow and longing, I tagged him, then quickly posted the photo.

I stared at my phone for several long moments, waiting for it to burn my hands as fate's way of telling me not to intervene with her plan. When it didn't, I finally let out the breath I'd been holding and placed the phone under my pillow, wanting to stay close to the only connection I had to him. It would have to do.

CHAPTER SEVEN

"ELLIE?" MILA CALLED OUT from the hallway the next morning, followed by a soft knock on my bedroom door. "Are you okay? It's after ten."

I continued lying in bed, staring at my phone, willing it to alert me that I had a new Instagram notification. I had checked it obsessively over the hours of sleeplessness that plagued me throughout the night. No notification ever came, other than some of my friends liking the photo. I didn't know what I expected to gain from tagging Dante in the post. I'd hoped for some sort of acknowledgment at least. Maybe he hadn't seen it. Maybe he no longer felt the same way. Worse, maybe he'd already moved on.

"I'm okay. You can come in," I said, sitting up in bed, checking my Instagram one more time.

The door creaked open and Mila popped her head in, then stepped into the room, placing a coffee mug on the nightstand. "Thought you could use this." She hesitated, scanning my appearance. "Rough night?"

I ran my hand over my face, secured my hair into a messy bun, then reached for the coffee. "More like rough life." My shoulders fell in defeat as I pulled my legs up to my stomach.

"What happened?" She sat on the edge of the bed, her concerned eyes seeming to analyze every inch of me. As grateful as I was for Mila's help over the past few weeks, I longed for the privacy that went along with having my own place, to be able to mend my broken heart in solitude.

"Nothing, Mila. Absolutely nothing." I sighed, turning my eyes to hers. "Maybe that's the problem. Maybe I thought…" I stared past her at the sun shining outside, a stark contrast to the darkness pervading my life. "I don't even know what I thought. But I certainly didn't think I would still be in the same spot I've been for over a month. I haven't accomplished anything I thought I would."

"These things take time," she encouraged, placing her hand on my arm. "Something will come along. I know it."

"I hope so." I raised the mug to my mouth, relishing in that first sip of coffee. Then, as if someone else were pulling the strings, I admitted, "I reached out to him."

Mila straightened her spine, her eyes widening. "What did you just say?"

I shrugged. "I reached out to him," I repeated, my voice lacking any excitement or energy. Life had beaten the hope out of me. Dante's failure to acknowledge me was the final straw.

She stared at me, her mouth agape. "Why? I thought—"

"I saw his face on the side of a bus yesterday," I explained. "Like, *really* saw it. It wasn't just someone who looked like him. It was a promo for his upcoming season." I shook my head, collecting my thoughts. "I haven't seen his face since I walked away from him at the airport in Rome. It hurt. I couldn't breathe, couldn't move, couldn't speak." My tone wavered as I struggled to talk through the heaviness in my throat. Giving voice to all these feelings I'd been dealing with made me feel raw, defenseless, broken, at complete odds with the woman I thought myself to be before this all began. "When I got home last night…I don't know. The pain was worse than it's ever been. So I took a peek at his Instagram account."

"Oh, Ellie," Mila sighed as she covered her mouth, an understanding look crossing her expression.

"Have you—"

"I wanted to tell you about the photos, but I didn't know how."

"It's probably better you didn't." I lowered my eyes, playing with the fabric of the duvet. "I was starting to think I imagined it all, that there was no way either one of us could have had these feelings for each other so soon. But after seeing his face on the side of that bus…" I wiped at my runny nose. "I wish I could just erase him from my heart because it hurts too much."

Mila swiftly pulled me into her arms. "You don't want to do that," she soothed, kissing the top of my head. "Remember how uptight and complacent you used to be? At least when it involved your personal life. Before Dante, you always did what your parents expected of you. Hell, you were about to marry a complete prick because that was what your *mother* wanted, not you. Dante opened your eyes to what life is really all about. It may hurt right now, but you don't want to erase him from your memory. You don't want to go back to being the Ellie you were before, do you?"

I subtly shook my head. "No. I don't."

"So you sent him a message on Instagram?" She released me, holding my gaze with her inquisitive eyes. "I thought you didn't want him to know how to get in touch with you."

"I didn't send him a message. I just tagged him in a post."

She studied me momentarily, then held out her hand. "Let me see it."

I hesitated briefly, but it didn't matter. She would eventually find it anyway. She was one of my few Instagram followers, although she didn't have much time for social media now that her days were preoccupied with taking care of two little ones.

Grabbing my phone, I opened the app, found the post in question, then handed it to her.

"Did he respond?" she asked, looking at the photo.

"Not yet. No like, no comment. Nothing." My shoulders fell as I pinched my lips together. "Maybe this is fate's way of telling me to stop messing with her plan."

"Or maybe it's all *part* of fate's plan." She narrowed her eyes on me, waggling her brows. "Maybe she wanted you to see his photo on that bus so you'd find your way to his Instagram account and finally reach out to him."

"I doubt it. I'm beginning to rethink my position on fate anyway." I blew out a long breath, defeated. "Maybe we're not meant to be together. Maybe this is what my life is supposed to be like. Maybe my relationship with Dante was meant to end. Maybe I was meant to wake up every day and watch his features slowly fade away. His voice. His scent. His arms. Until, one day, they're only a distant memory." I closed my eyes, fighting back the tears forming at the thought. "I wish they'd just be a distant memory already."

Mila pulled me into her arms again. "You don't mean that, Ellie. It may hurt right now, but it'll work itself out."

I wiped my cheeks. "I don't see how, but thanks for your encouragement." I pulled away from Mila, taking a long sip of my coffee now that it had a chance to cool off. "God, what's wrong with me?" I laughed through my tears. "I never used to cry. Now I can't stop."

"It's because you finally care enough about someone to know what heartache feels like. Dante made you human, Ellie. Something you never learned from your uncaring, perfect parents. Being human means your heart may feel a few cracks and breaks along the way. But I'll be the first to tell you that it's far better than going through life as an unfeeling, heartless robot."

"I guess you're right," I muttered, bringing the mug back to my lips when a loud ding tore through the room.

We immediately snapped our wide eyes to each

other, my breath caught in my throat. I quickly placed my coffee on the nightstand and scrambled for my phone, my heart racing in my chest. It could just be an email from yet another job prospect telling me they weren't interested, but something about this moment made me think it wasn't. It made no sense, but I knew in my heart it was Dante.

Unlocking my screen with frantic hands, I opened my Instagram, a smile crossing my face when I saw that not only did Dante Luciano start following me, but he'd also mentioned me in a post.

"What is it?" Mila asked excitedly, bouncing on the bed.

When I clicked on the photo, all the tension melted off my body, hope filling me once more. Maybe all was not yet lost. I briefly closed my eyes, inhaling deeply, allowing the photo and words below it to bathe me in comfort that everything was going to be okay, that fate knew what she was doing.

"I don't get it," Mila remarked, peering over my shoulder.

"That's the bar at his restaurant in Rome... Inferno." I stared dreamily at the photo of a suit jacket laid over a barstool, a single red rose on top of it. I could almost smell the garlic, tomatoes, and wine. I could almost hear the dull murmur of polite conversation. I could almost feel his heated stare on me. "I sat on that exact barstool the night he approached me. When we left to go to the Trevi Fountain, he draped that jacket over my shoulders to keep me warm."

"What does the caption say?"

"'Whoever loved that loved not at first sight?' - William Shakespeare, *As You Like It.*"

"That's beautiful, Ellie."

I simply nodded, clutching my phone against my chest. It was such a small thing, but the photo, the quote... We didn't have to send meaningless emails back and forth detailing the mundane events of our day. We could communicate in a way I never expected. We could share our lives, our thoughts, our love with a photo and words that only we would be able to fully understand.

I quickly shot up from the bed, scanning my surroundings. I needed to respond, to tell him how I felt, how much I missed him. An idea popped into my head. I rushed down the stairs and into the kitchen, Mila behind me every step of the way.

"What are you looking for?" she asked as I rummaged through the cabinets.

I stood on my toes, craning my neck to see what was on the top shelf. "That antique tea set you have... Where is it?"

"Hold on." She headed out of the kitchen and into the guest room adjacent to the family room, returning a few seconds later with the wooden box. Placing it on the island, she unlatched it. I pulled out two tea cups, arranging them on the saucers before adding a few decorative elements — napkins, silver spoons, rose petals I stole from one of her floral arrangements. Once it looked right, I snapped the photo.

"I get it," Mila said, understanding replacing the confusion on her face. "The tea room."

Recalling exactly what had happened in that tea room, details I still hadn't shared with her, my cheeks heated. I quickly looked away so she wouldn't push for more information, and captioned the photo. I considered scouring Google for an appropriate Shakespeare quote, but decided to use something a bit more personal instead.

"I fell... Just a little at first..." - D.L., June
"Then all the way..." - E.C., Present Day

After I tagged him, I hit post, hoping it wouldn't be long before I received a response. Thankfully, only a few minutes passed before he tagged me in a photo of the Trevi Fountain at night. To most people, it wouldn't appear to be anything more than one of Rome's most beautiful spots. To me, it was everything, particularly when I read the caption.

Sempre e per sempre.

There was only one way for me to answer that. I ran upstairs and into my room, Mila sprinting to catch up. Every inch of me seemed to glow, a feeling of weightlessness coursing through me at the confirmation that Dante was still in the world, that he still thought about me...that he still loved me. Sifting through my purse, I found the Euro coin that never made its way into the fountain, the Euro coin that told me to get on that plane and leave Dante. Placing it in my hand, I snapped a photo and posted it, using the same caption Dante had.

"*Sempre e per sempre*," Mila murmured over my shoulder, reading my words. "What does it mean?"

"Always and forever."

She wrapped her arms around me, kissing my temple. "Told you it would all work out."

CHAPTER EIGHT

AND SO BEGAN MY "love letters" to Dante in the form of Instagram posts. Over the following weeks, we shared at least one photo a day, along with a caption about love...some notable, others not. We didn't directly come out and ask questions or have any sort of conversation. We didn't need to. The photos we shared said everything we wanted. We spoke in a language only we could interpret. My world finally seemed a little brighter knowing Dante was out there, thinking of me just as my thoughts were consumed by him.

But, just like everything in my life, I knew that brightness would eventually grow dim. And it did on a Friday in August as I drove to my parents' house for my mother's weekly dinner party.

As I came to a stop at a red light a few miles from their house, my phone dinged with a new notification. When I reached into my purse and grabbed it, I saw Dante had tagged me in a new Instagram post. I grinned, thinking he must be missing me a little bit more than usual today, considering this was his fourth post. But when I saw the photo he tagged me in, my heart fell, a chill enveloping me. I had been dreading this, wondering about it, but didn't have the courage to ask. Now I wished I had, if for no other reason than to be able to say a proper goodbye.

It was a beautiful image, one hand lying on top of another. The one on the bottom was more feminine, obviously belonging to someone who had lived more years. The other was younger, more masculine, one I still occasionally imagined wrapped around my own hand. My breath caught when I read the caption.

> *"The valiant never taste of death but once."* - *William Shakespeare, Julius Caesar. RIP Mama.*

I covered my mouth with my hand, hiding my quivering chin as my eyes welled with tears. Dante said she had three months. It had only been two. I didn't want to believe she was gone.

Looking up from the photo, I glanced at the cars surrounding me. People talked animatedly on their phones or tapped their steering wheels impatiently, continuing on, as if the world were the same as it was just moments ago. But I knew it would never be the same. Not for Dante. Not for his family. And not for me. It didn't matter that I'd only spent a few hours with his mother. She'd opened her heart, her home, her life to me, knowing who I was, knowing my family, but still welcoming me. My world seemed a little sadder, a little darker, a little less forgiving now that Gabriella Luciano was no longer in it. I could only imagine how Dante was coping with the loss.

I instantly recalled the image of him resting his forehead on hers as they shared a moment in her house in Italy. I was grateful to have been able to witness their love, a love I thought only existed in the movies and on television. Their connection gave me hope that I'd have something similar with my own child one day. I'd forever be grateful to Gabriella for opening my mind and heart to the possibility of having a family, something I never wanted before.

I returned my eyes to my phone, tempted to shoot off a direct message to Dante, but stopped myself. Part of me liked the idea that we weren't speaking directly to one another, that we chose to bear our hearts, our souls, through photos of the world around us. What inspired us. What brought us joy. What caused us pain.

When the light turned green, I quickly shoved my phone back into my purse and stepped on the gas, losing myself in my thoughts as I continued driving toward my parents' house. How was I supposed to respond to this news? Should I get on a flight to Italy? I didn't have the money for that, and my credit card was maxed out. Was this fate's way of telling me to swallow my pride and ask my father for a loan? I doubted she'd want me to do that, not when the coin landed on heads for a reason. She wouldn't send me back here to free myself from my parents' shadow just to grovel for money. As much as I wanted to wrap my arms around Dante and offer him the comfort he needed, I had to put my trust in fate. If I were meant to go to Italy to be with him, fate would make it happen.

Resolved, I wiped my cheeks, then pinched them so it didn't look like I'd been crying. The last thing I wanted was to give my mother any ammunition to use against me, although I no longer had any desire to go to the dinner party and listen to everyone drone on about the latest gossip.

As I drove, I glanced to my right, noticing a Catholic Church I never had in all my years of driving this very road. I quickly slammed on my brakes, my tires squealing as I veered into the parking lot. I found a spot and killed the engine, sitting in silence for a moment. I had asked for a sign. Perhaps this was it. I wasn't even sure if this was allowed, if you could just walk into a church anytime you wanted, but I felt compelled to be here.

Smoothing the lines of my dress, I stepped out of the car and walked across the lot toward a set of stairs leading up to a pair of large wooden doors. I paused at the bottom, craning my head to peer at the cross on the steeple. The breeze picked up, my hair blowing in front of my face. I could almost smell the same sweet aroma that was in the air at Gabriella's house in Italy. It was probably just my brain playing tricks on me, but part of me liked to think she was here with me, telling me I was on the right path. Her words the night I met her resounded in my mind, as if she were whispering in my ear...

What is meant to be will be.

Before I stepped foot on that plane to Rome, I never understood why people followed religion or believed in what I considered to be ridiculous ideas, such as fate. It seemed like just an excuse to put all accountability for your actions on some higher power, to not be held to answer for your own failings or misgivings. But it made sense now. Sometimes life just sucked and you wanted to believe there was a reason for everything. Sometimes you needed to allow a higher power to take the wheel for a minute. Sometimes you just needed to be reminded that the universe was a huge place and you were nothing more than a tiny speck in it.

I continued up the stairs, then pulled one of the doors open and walked inside. Silence and serenity instantly surrounded me. Gone was the noise of cars, honking horns, and yelling voices. In here, it was just me…and God. I couldn't say goodbye to Gabriella in person. But I could do it here, and I knew she'd hear me.

I stepped farther into the church, which was empty, apart from a few nuns praying in the pews. One of them must have sensed my presence because she did the sign of the cross and slowly rose. When she emerged into the aisle, she genuflected before the altar, then turned around, heading toward me.

I considered leaving, thinking I may be intruding, but I felt compelled to do this, to light a candle for Gabriella.

"Good evening, dear," the woman said kindly. She wore a dark habit, a wooden cross hanging from her neck. She had thin lips and dark eyes, little wisps of white hair visible from under her head covering. "Have you come for confession?"

I opened my mouth and shook my head as I peered at her, my brow wrinkling. "I'm sorry. I'm not Catholic. I just…" I paused, drawing in a deep breath. "I just learned someone I cared for passed away. She was

Catholic, so I wanted to light a candle for her. I think she would have wanted me to do that."

The nun reached out and grabbed my hand, squeezing it. "Of course. Come with me." She kept my hand enclosed in hers as she led me into the sanctuary and toward a stained glass window depicting the first station of the cross. Below it sat a devotional area, just like at Dante's church in Italy. But only a few candles had been lit here, unlike in Italy where many had been burning, even early in the morning. This was yet another reminder of the different cultures we grew up in and came from.

I paused as we approached the area, then knelt on the cushioned kneeler in front of me. The nun handed me one of the long matches and I struck it. A flame immediately sparked to life. I held it up to one of the wicks, watching the flame dance in front of me as I lit the candle.

"Do you mind if I light a candle for your friend…?" The nun's eyebrows rose.

"Gabriella," I said, then nodded, giving her permission.

"What a beautiful name." She joined me, striking a match, lighting yet another candle.

"She was a beautiful person, a beautiful soul."

She simply nodded, then folded her hands in front of her, leaning her head on them, mimicking the pose I found Dante in that day in Italy. "Would you like to pray with me?" she asked when she sensed me studying her.

"I don't know how," I answered honestly.

"That's okay." She gave me an encouraging smile. I placed my hands in front of me, mirroring her pose, closing my eyes. "Eternal rest grant unto Gabriella, O Lord, and let perpetual light shine upon her. May the souls of all the faithful departed, through the mercy of God, rest in peace." She paused, then added, "Amen."

Unsure what else to do, I repeated, "Amen."

I lifted my head, staring at the candles for several more minutes. The chill I felt when I first learned of Gabriella's passing had miraculously been replaced by a feeling of warmth and comfort. I hoped this was her way of letting me know she was okay, that she wasn't in pain anymore, that she would look out for Dante until our paths finally crossed again.

Drawing in a long breath, I slowly stood, meeting the nun's eyes. "Thank you."

"Of course, dear." She raised herself to her feet. "Our door is always open."

I nodded slightly, then began to turn, but stopped myself, facing her once more. "Do you mind if I take a photo of the candles? She was my friend's mother. They're in Italy. I just... I just want him to know I was thinking about him. That even though I couldn't be there to say goodbye in person—"

She placed her hand on my arm, cutting me off. "Of course."

"Thank you." I smiled, pulling my phone out of my purse. Making sure to capture the moment as best as I could, I snapped a photo of the two candles we lit.

~~~~~~~~~~

ONCE I WAS BACK in the car, I steered it in the opposite direction of my parents' house. I didn't want to be around them. Not tonight. Instead, I found myself pulling into the parking lot of an Italian restaurant in Woodland Hills and headed into the bar. Enjoying a glass of wine probably didn't sound like an appropriate way to cope with someone's passing, but I knew enough to know Gabriella wouldn't have wanted me to mourn her. She would have wanted me to do something to celebrate her life. And what better way to do that than to have a glass of wine and good food?

After I placed my order with the bartender and a glass of wine appeared in front of me, I pulled my phone out and opened the Instagram app, trying to come up with a caption that properly conveyed what I wanted to say. I stared at the photo of the candles, unsure how to put my feelings into words. Sometimes simple was better. Sometimes you just needed to speak from the heart. So that was what I did.

> *"Thank you for showing me what love looks like. Your light will always shine in my heart because of that."*

I studied it, hoping it was good enough, then tagged Dante in the photo, posting it. I put my phone on the bar and took a sip of my wine.

"Ellie?" a voice said.

I turned to my left, seeing a man with dirty blond hair, sky blue eyes, and a perfectly tailored suit approach the bar. "Quinn?"

"It *is* you," he breathed, taking the empty seat next to me. "I thought it was, but the hair threw me for a loop."

I laughed slightly, toying with one of my locks. "I changed it back to its natural color."

"Nice," he said, signaling the bartender. "It looks good on you."

"What are you doing here? Woodland Hills is a bit far from O'Connell and Greene, isn't it?" I asked after he placed his drink order.

I met Quinn my first month as an associate at my old law firm. He was opposing counsel on a case and had proven to be quite the worthy adversary. However, he was still no match for my tenacity and drive, not to mention the fact that I routinely worked eighty-hour weeks because I didn't like being home with Brock. Despite representing clients with opposing viewpoints, we formed a friendship.

"I quit about a year ago and started my own firm in Encino. I got tired of someone else telling me which cases to take and making me ask some of my clients to mortgage their houses just to pay our legal fees. I was just out here for a meeting." He nodded in appreciation as the bartender placed his beer in front of him. "How about you?" he asked hesitantly after taking a sip. He'd probably heard I was fired. Everyone seemed to know about that, considering getting fired from Sullivan,

Sullivan & Grace was the equivalent of being blacklisted, as I'd learned over the past several weeks.

"Oh, you know…" I smiled sweetly. "Stood my politician fiancé up at the altar, so now no law firm will touch me with a ten-foot pole."

He slowly shook his head, his lips pinching together as they formed into a small, sympathetic smile.

"No one seems to care I have a law degree from Georgetown and worked at one of the top law firms in the state. I'm still not qualified for their open positions." My voice oozed with sarcasm before my contrived smile fell, my expression becoming despondent. "Maybe it's a sign I'm not supposed to be doing this."

The atmosphere between us grew thick as I stared at all the bottles of liquor behind the bar, not really seeing anything. I'd never actually admitted that to myself before. While I'd grown extremely frustrated with the fact that not one single firm had called to set up an interview, I still pushed forward. How much longer could I do this? Maybe I needed to look elsewhere, do something different before I ended up flipping burgers at a fast food restaurant. I just didn't know if I was good at anything else. I'd never done anything else. I never trained for anything else. This was the plan for my life since day one. What was I supposed to do now?

I toyed with my wine glass, swirling it on the bar, straightening my shoulders. I didn't want Quinn to pity me. He'd successfully broken away from one of the top law firms in the state, even though he was only five years older than me. I could do the same. Maybe running into him was fate's way of telling me I should just start my own practice.

"I can't pay you what you're used to making." Quinn's voice cut into my thoughts.

I practically choked on my wine as I shot my wide eyes to him. "Wait. What?"

"And it's definitely not as glamorous as Sullivan. There's no monthly stipend or company car. Your office will probably be no bigger than a bathroom, and you'll be handling a lot of workers' comp and social security cases. It's a job, though."

I studied him, wondering if I heard him correctly or if my mind was playing tricks on me. "What exactly are you saying, Quinn?"

He laughed slightly. "Ellie, you're a brilliant attorney. You take no prisoners in negotiations. I was going over my firm's caseload earlier and came to the conclusion I need to add another attorney. It just so happens you're an attorney who needs a job. What do you say?"

I blinked repeatedly, my jaw becoming slack as my brain struggled to tell my mouth to move, my voice box to vibrate and make sound.

"Ellie?" he asked.

I quickly snapped out of my stupor and hopped off my barstool, flinging my arms around his neck. "Thank you. Thank you. Thank you!" I squealed in an uncharacteristic move, but I had no idea how else to express my overwhelming gratitude to this man. Dante believed everything happened for a reason, including his daughter's death. Maybe fate gave me a reason to skip my parents' party so I'd run into Quinn.

"Does this mean you'll take the job?" He chuckled.

I stepped back, releasing my hold on him, a huge smile on my face. "When can I start?"

CHAPTER NINE

"**Y**OU DO KNOW YOU get paid the same regardless of how many hours you work, correct?" Quinn's voice cut through the silence as I took notes on a deposition I'd been looking over.

I glanced up to see him leaning on the doorjamb of my new office. He wasn't lying when he said it wouldn't be any bigger than a bathroom, but it didn't matter. It was a job. While I never saw myself practicing in workers' compensation or social security law, it was a welcome change of pace from corporate law, and he'd given me flexibility to branch out into other areas in the future.

"I know," I responded, smiling. "It's just a new area for me, so I'm trying to get caught up on procedure and case law."

"You'll figure it out, Ellie." He winked. "Why don't you call it a night? Most of the staff gets together at The Iron Tap for Happy Hour on Thursdays. You should come."

I hesitated. I'd planned to go pick out some new furniture for the apartment I just signed a lease on. Now that I had a job with a steady income, I used the rest of my savings to put down the first month's rent and security deposit on a small studio apartment in a complex a mile or so from the office. I even bought a car.

Mila had insisted it was okay if I stayed with them and continued to use Steven's car a little bit longer, but there was this part of me that thought if I finally had a job, a place of my own, and a car, I'd be that much closer to fate bringing Dante and me back together.

"Come on," Quinn urged, sensing my reluctance. "You need a break. Based on your reputation over at Sullivan, I knew you were a bit of a workaholic, but I didn't think you'd be pulling sixteen-hour days your second week here."

"I don't mind. It keeps me out of trouble," I joked, flashing him a fabricated smile.

He crossed his arms in front of his chest, narrowing his eyes at me. Based on the look on his face, I had a feeling he wasn't going to leave unless I agreed to go with him.

"Fine," I sighed. "Let me just finish reading this deposition and I'll meet you there, okay? Fifteen minutes."

His smile brightened. "Perfect. Are you okay to lock up?"

"You bet."

"See you in a bit, Ellie." He pushed off the doorjamb and disappeared down the hallway.

I returned to the papers in front of me, trying to get back into the groove, but my concentration was elsewhere. After about ten minutes of reading words that felt like a foreign language, nothing sinking in, I pushed back from my desk, grabbed my purse, and headed out of the office.

Waving goodnight to the security guard in the lobby, I stepped into the warm California night. The bar was about five blocks up the street and I considered driving, but it was a pleasant evening. I'd spent too much time cooped up in that office trying to get caught up. I could use the fresh air.

I heard my phone beep as I passed a coffee shop and reached into my purse, pulling it out. When I saw Dante had tagged me in an Instagram post, those butterflies that had taken up residence in my stomach began flapping their relentless wings. After learning of his mother's death, I'd given him space to mourn her, and the posts had stopped for a few days while he did so. But a week ago, they started again, his words and images even more loving, endearing, and sensual, if that were at all possible.

Slowing my steps, I opened the app, biting back the grin struggling to break free as I stared at the exterior shot of the museum in Rome where we'd attended the gala. Memories of what we'd done in one of the bathrooms flooded back and a warmth rushed over me, my cheeks flushing. Then I read the caption.

"Can one desire too much of a good thing?" - *William Shakespeare, As You Like It.*

"Oh, Dante," I exhaled. "Why do you have to be so perfect? And so far away?" Looking up, I stared into space, trying to come up with a proper response, when I noticed a familiar car pull up and park a block ahead.

At first, I didn't think much of it. A black Mercedes wasn't exactly a rare car in this town. But when I saw my father step out of the driver's seat and hurry into a shady-looking bar, my curiosity got the best of me. I knew what I was about to do may be incredibly stupid, but I couldn't help but wonder if maybe I was supposed to leave work early so I could see him. Maybe fate knew I was struggling for answers as to whether or not he was involved in Lilly's death. If I followed him into the bar, maybe I would get those answers. So that was what I did.

The entire place was dimly lit, the perfect spot for someone who didn't want to be seen. The air was dank with the faint aroma of stale cigarette smoke, even though I doubted anyone had smoked in here in years. Green carpeting covered the floor, the shade matching the color of the felt on the few pool tables toward the back of the small room. A u-shaped bar made up the center, a dozen or so booths lining the walls. I noticed my father sitting alone in a booth at the very rear of the bar, what I assumed to be a scotch in front of him.

My suspicions only increased with each passing moment that I remained in this place, discreetly studying my father's demeanor. He had no reason to be in Encino. His office was located in downtown LA, and he lived in Calabasas. The only reason he was even in California on a Thursday was because the Senate wasn't in session this month. He was normally only home Fridays through Mondays. Given everything I knew about him, it seemed strange he would be at a crappy bar in this town…unless he was up to something.

"Can I help you?" a scruff voice called out, and I quickly snapped out of my thoughts. Stepping toward the bar, I shielded my face with my hair, hoping my father hadn't seen me.

"Whiskey and soda, please." I hastily fished my wallet out of my purse, doing my best not to draw too much attention to myself.

"You got it." The bartender grabbed a bottle off the counter and poured the dark liquor into a rocks glass. After adding a bit of soda, he set it down in front of me. I handed him a $20 bill.

"Keep the change."

"Rough day?"

"Something like that," I mumbled in a curt voice, giving off the impression that I wanted to be left alone. Thankfully, the bartender picked up on that. I retreated from him and kept my eyes downcast as I headed down the empty bar, hoisting myself onto one of the stools closer to where my father sat. I carefully glanced over my shoulder at him, sensing his unease and frustration.

For as long as I could remember, he'd been confident, assured, put-together. The way he constantly toyed with the glass in front of him, as if needing something to do with his hands, made me think he was slowly losing control of everything.

I'd only been sitting there a few seconds when the door opened again and a man I estimated to be about fifty hurried inside, a crazed expression on his face. His dark hair was disheveled, his clothes giving the impression that he didn't care much about his appearance. He could have just been another local needing something to take the edge off after a bad day, but I couldn't ignore the feeling in my gut that this man was the reason my father was here.

The man scanned the bar, his eyes eventually landing on my father. He immediately rushed toward him and ducked into the booth, keeping his head down. His legs nervously bounced as he bit his nails and glanced over his shoulder, jittery, maybe even a little paranoid.

I quickly snapped my attention back to the Dodgers game playing on the TV hanging over the bar, straightening my spine as I took a sip of my drink. I did my best to keep an ear turned toward my father and this mystery man, hoping to overhear their discussion. I feared if I got any closer, he'd recognize me.

"I've been looking through the reports from that night," the man said.

"You need to stop torturing yourself like this. What good could rehashing that tragic day do?"

"Because nothing about it seems right," the man retorted, then lowered his voice even more. "With all the shit she had been doing… It's just a bit suspicious. Cynthia…" He trailed off with a quiver, then recovered. "She had so much to live for. She wasn't suicidal. She wasn't depressed. Given the circumstances, she'd remained surprisingly positive…a lot more positive than most people would be in her situation. I just can't believe she would have taken her own life, not when she was willing to put that life on the line to do what she believed was right."

My heart seemed to echo in my ears as I leaned closer, glued to this man's every word. Recalling the background check I found at Brock's, I realized this man must have been talking about Cynthia Edelman and the night she died. This had to be her ex-husband, Brian, father of her two teenage girls, all of whom she left behind when she allegedly committed suicide. But after overhearing that phone call in Italy and going through the files in Brock's office, I had a feeling it wasn't a suicide at all.

"Brian," my father sighed. "I didn't want to believe it at first, either. But the medical examiner and the crime scene techs found absolutely no evidence of foul play, no evidence anyone else was in that room. Apart from her own, no fingerprints were found on the gun she used, the gun she just so happened to have bought the previous day. The security cameras also didn't pick up anyone going near her office around that time. I know how it looks, given what she was involved in. Her death was shocking, but I assure you, it was by her own hand, no one else's."

There was a brief pause before either man spoke again. "When I met her for coffee that morning to discuss how much longer she thought it necessary for the girls to stay with me, never did I think it would be the last time I'd see her," Brian stated, his tone even, flat, lacking any emotion. "I was so broken up at the time that I didn't question anything. In the back of my mind, I feared this day would come, especially when she said she was planning to come forward with whatever she found out. But now that nearly six months have passed, I can't help but wonder if you're lying to me."

I knew he was lying, especially after finding those surveillance photos of my father walking into Barnes Pharmaceuticals mere minutes before Cynthia had taken her life. It was possible there could be another explanation, but my father had never given me a single reason to trust him. I wasn't about to start now.

"I have no reason to lie to you, Brian," my father replied evenly. "I cared about Cynthia, too. Her death hit me hard."

I struggled not to laugh at his words. It hit him hard all right. Hard enough that he'd want to cover up his involvement in it. I didn't know how he did it, but not one single security camera in the building picked up on my father entering that evening. But someone did...the same man who took the photo of my father rushing through the front doors just after eight that evening, then another of him leaving approximately twenty minutes later. The same photos Brock had in his desk. If it weren't for those, I wouldn't have known he'd even been there. No one would. Who took them? Why did Brock have them? Why hadn't he gone to the police with this? And who's side was he on?

"It didn't seem that way," Brian remarked.

"You were a wreck, Brian. Someone needed to step in and get things done."

"And you figured, because of your past with Cynthia,

that man should be you?" He paused, then continued. "She told me everything about—"

"I had a feeling she would at some point," my father interrupted with a heavy sigh. "It was only a matter of time until it came up."

I strained to hear better, wondering what his past with Cynthia entailed. How long had they known each other?

"The reason she did what she did all those years ago was because of *you*, so people wouldn't realize you weren't this golden boy, this beacon of morality who was going to clean up dirty politics. But I know the truth. You're just like everyone else. You'd gladly destroy a person's hopes and dreams in order to achieve your own. You've destroyed our family, a family Cynthia wanted for years. She would *never* leave them. She would *never* kill herself..." He trailed off, a quiver in his voice.

When I heard a slight rustling, I peered over my shoulder, watching Brian stand from the booth.

"Despite what you're telling me, what the reports say, I know she didn't take her own life. I'm going to get to the bottom of what happened, and I don't care what it takes to do that. I *will* bring Cynthia's killer to justice, even if it's by my own hand." He quickly spun around and began walking away.

"Brian, wait," my father called out. I discreetly stole a glimpse at him, watching as he licked his lips, as if debating what he was about to do. Then he sighed, resigned. "She's not dead."

Brian immediately stopped in his tracks, slowly turning around. Disbelief and anger rolled over his features, the distaste he harbored for my father as clear as day, his lips curled, his eyes narrowed.

"Don't you think I've been through enough, that the kids have been through enough?" he asked in a quiet but firm voice. "No child should have to sit through her mother's funeral, then pretend she's happy when her date picks her up for her senior prom. This was supposed to be the best time in Maggie's life. Finishing high school. Starting college. Instead, I've had to listen to her crying in her room every day about how much she misses her mother. So don't you *dare* stand there and tell me it's all been for nothing, that this is just another one of your mind games, a way to stop me from finally going to the police with what I know, which I should have done back in March."

"Please, Brian…" My father stepped toward him, his brows gathered in, a pleading look on his face. "If you'll just sit down and listen to what I have to say, I'll tell you everything I know. Then, if you still feel the need to go to the police, I'll drive you there myself."

A moment of quiet contemplation passed while Brian seemed to weigh his options. Then he headed back toward the booth, retaking his seat.

"If she's not dead, why would the medical examiner say she was?"

"He owed me a favor. The hardest part was trying to convince you that you didn't need to see her body. Insisting her face wasn't recognizable because of the gunshot wound helped."

Brian closed his eyes, soaking in my father's version of events, still wary of his trustworthiness.

"Someone must have figured out what Cynthia was about to do, so they put a target on her back. After a car nearly rammed into her as she crossed the street that day after meeting with you, she knew what she needed to do. A friend of mine, who is very good at making people disappear, agreed to help. Someone wanted Cynthia dead, so that's what we gave them. It was the only way to keep you and your girls safe. If they thought she ran, they'd come after you and your children. We couldn't let that happen. Faking her death was the only option."

"You honestly expect me to believe this story? Because a car almost hit her when she was crossing the street?"

"You don't have to believe anything, but you should. It's the truth."

"Where's your proof?"

My father sighed heavily. "I don't have any."

Brian shook his head, his voice filled with disgust. "I can't help but think you're blowing smoke up my ass so I won't look into her death anymore, so I won't find out the truth that *you* were responsible for it. Aside from me, you were the only person who knew what she was about to do, who she was about to meet." He leaned closer, his face less than an inch from my father's. "She trusted you. She kept your secret for nearly three decades. When this all began, you were the first person she went to. But now…maybe *you're* the person behind it all."

"Nothing could be further from the truth. I want to help her, not hurt her."

"Then tell me where she is. If your version of events is to be believed, this is one way to prove it." He leaned back in the booth, crossing his arms in front of his chest.

My father blew out a frustrated breath, lowering his head. "I can't. I don't know where she is."

Brian threw his head back, laughing sarcastically. "I don't know what kind of game you're playing here, but—"

"This is *not* a game. It was the only way. We needed to make these people believe she died. More importantly, we needed *you* to believe she died. If you weren't mourning her, whoever's behind this would have grown suspicious. So we did what was necessary. We cut all communication between us. She knows to stay hidden until this is all over."

"Isn't that convenient?"

"No. It's the truth."

"You wouldn't know what truth was if it slapped you in the face." Brian stood again, glowering down at my father. "Your entire life has been built on one lie after another, on manipulating people so they do what you want. The bottom will eventually drop. I just hope I'm around to see you finally pay for everything you've done throughout your miserable excuse of an existence."

He abruptly turned and rushed out of the bar. This time, my father made no move to stop him. Instead, he drew in a deep breath, rubbing his temples. I returned my eyes to the uneventful baseball game on the television, trying to make sense out of what I'd just overheard.

My father wanted Brian to think Cynthia *wasn't* dead, but why? So Brian wouldn't look into her death and discover that he was behind it? So he wouldn't find out she didn't commit suicide as he wanted him and the rest of the world to believe? And what was this secret of my father's she'd been keeping?

I agreed with Brian. It was much easier to believe Cynthia was dead than the story my father concocted about her being in hiding. Not to mention, I knew something Brian didn't…that my father had sent her threatening emails, ordering her to thwart Dante's attention or suffer the consequences. Was my father playing both sides? Did he pretend to be a friend when Cynthia came to him with a problem, then put a target on her back when she confessed she was going to finally go public with what was going on? But what *was* going on? What information would my father kill for to keep quiet? And how did he even know Cynthia?

I felt a slight breeze behind me and glanced to my right, watching my father's silhouette disappear out the door. I waited for a moment, taking the time to finish my drink. Once my glass was empty, I stood, adjusted my suit, then left. Stepping onto the sidewalk, I looked up and down the street, feeling exposed, wondering if someone knew what I'd been doing, if someone was going to come after me now that *I* knew something.

Just as I passed an alley on my way back to the office

to do some more digging into Cynthia Edelman's death so I could corroborate or disprove my father's story, a hand unexpectedly grabbed onto my arm. I screamed, flailing against the figure pulling me into the shadows. A rough hand covered my mouth, trying to silence my cries.

"Shh. It's okay," a familiar voice soothed.

I stopped struggling, my breathing slowing as I craned my head and peered into the eyes of the person holding me. Blinking repeatedly, I freed myself of his grasp, smoothing the lines of my suit.

"Dad? What are—"

"I know you were listening in on my conversation in there."

I remained silent, not making any excuse for my behavior. If anyone needed to explain themselves, it was him.

"It's okay," he assured me. "I would have done the same thing if I saw my father park his car in an area of the city he typically wouldn't be in and walk into a crappy bar."

"What you said…," I began, squaring my shoulders, holding my head high. It always worked during negotiations when I wanted to appear more confident and assured than I felt on the inside. I hoped it worked here, too. After what I just heard, I needed to have the upper hand to get to the truth. "Is it true?" I crossed my arms in front of my chest, my eyes narrowed, wanting him to see he couldn't bullshit me.

"Every word of it," he answered in a soft tone, his

eyes imploring.

"Where is she?" I pushed, relentless. "And what's this secret of yours she's been keeping?"

His breath hitched. "Ellie…" His shoulders fell as he shook his head. "I…"

"You can waffle all you want, but I'm done with the bullshit excuses you give me every week that you're just trying to protect me by keeping me in the dark." I leaned into him. "I *will* get to the bottom of this. I won't stop until I've uncovered everything you've been involved in, every place you've been, every person you've ever had dealings with, every back room conversation you've ever been a part of. I'll know it all, including whether or not Cynthia truly is in 'hiding'," I said, using air quotes, hoping he'd see how much I struggled to believe his version of events. "So just come clean. Otherwise, I'll go to the press with what I've been able to figure out on my own so far. Negative publicity in an election year is never a good thing."

He ran his hand over his tired face, seeming to lack the vigor and vitality he usually exuded. He appeared worn, beaten down. I wondered if maybe he *was* telling the truth. That maybe he put his own neck on the line to help Cynthia hide from all of this. Then again, this man had spent the past thirty years in the political arena. He had perfected the art of lying to the American people. Lying to his daughter was no different.

"I met Cynthia when I went to D.C. after winning my first election thirty years ago," he explained, resigned. "She was a senior at George Washington University and doing a congressional internship. She had a brilliant mind. I knew she'd grow into a force to be reckoned with on the Hill, but that wasn't the direction life took her. Instead, after finishing law school, she worked for a few prestigious firms in Chicago, then signed on as in-house counsel for Barnes Pharmaceuticals. When they relocated their home office to California, she went with them. We lost touch over the years as we both built our careers. It wasn't until about seven years ago that we ran into each other out of the blue. I figured another twenty-something years would go by before we saw each other again, but this time, it was only a few months before she showed up at my office here in California."

"What did she want?"

He swallowed hard. "She was being blackmailed. Said someone found out about something that had happened years ago and she was being forced to engage in violations of the ethical code to keep this information a secret and her family alive."

I licked my lips. In the back of my mind, I wondered if my father was the one blackmailing her. "How so?"

"She was told to do whatever necessary to make sure a certain drug, which she refused to share with me at the time, made it to market and stayed there. I told her I'd help try to figure out who was behind it. I had a few suspicions, but nothing came of them. All correspondence and threats came in the form of untraceable envelopes sent to her home address. No fingerprints were left. Any phone calls were from a burner phone. They were good. They knew what they were doing."

His praise for their efficiency at not getting caught made me sick to my stomach. I wanted to ask about the emails he and Cynthia had exchanged, but decided against it. My father wasn't aware I knew about those. I needed to keep a few tricks up my sleeve…for now.

"And this secret?"

"I… I can't tell you. Not yet. Not until I know no harm will come to anyone because of it."

"Even all these years later?" I lifted a brow, my voice heavy with disbelief.

"Yes, Ellie. Even all these years later." He gazed upon me fondly, his hand twitching, as if wanting to reach out and caress my skin. "Until I can figure out what's going on, you have to trust me that this secret is not illegal. It's just something that may paint me in a…somewhat different light."

"Trust," I scoffed. "That's an interesting word coming from you."

"I know I've never given you a reason to believe me, and that's on me. I take full responsibility for not being the best father to you. But, for the first time in your life, I need you to take a leap of faith and trust me. I promise, I will eventually tell you everything, but not yet."

"What information was she going to share with Dante?" I pressed, narrowing my gaze at him.

"When he started calling around, asking about a particular drug they manufactured, the drug she was being blackmailed over, Cynthia got nervous that he'd bring too much unwelcome attention to the company. It goes without saying that these people wouldn't look too kindly upon that. Luckily, she was able to convince him that it tested well, that there was no evidence to suggest there was anything wrong with the drug in question. But the guilt started to eat her up, particularly when she learned what happened to his daughter. She couldn't imagine being in his shoes, so she began to look at the reports a little more closely. A small number of patients who had taken the drug in question did die, but reports didn't say with certainty it was because of the drug. Even if the FDA looked into it, they wouldn't think anything was wrong.

"She continued analyzing the reports, charting the deaths. There was a slight increase over a short period of time roughly six years ago, around the time she began getting the threats. She concluded that perhaps a batch had been contaminated. It was a newer drug, so she theorized that maybe the CEO or someone else higher up was the one threatening her, considering the board and majority shareholders stood to gain millions, if not billions, of dollars by the success of this drug."

"And lose even more if it was pulled off the shelves."

"Exactly. But the numbers indicated this was a small batch of potentially contaminated drugs. It wouldn't require a massive recall. So she then started looking into other drugs with reports of deaths and charted those. She came up with a list of over a dozen that also exhibited a slight increase in deaths during a short period of time, then evened out. She wouldn't tell me exactly what drugs were on the list, said she didn't want to put any more lives in jeopardy. After receiving a threat about eliminating the 'Dante Luciano problem', she said she was done playing their game, that she was going to go public with what she knew, consequences be damned, and use Dante to try to diminish any potential blowback on her family."

"And her claim that this corruption went all the way to the head of the FDA?" I lifted a brow.

"Just something I told her to use to convince Dante to meet with her. James and I have always been close. I knew about his affair with Gabriella and Dante's animosity toward him."

I didn't react, simply absorbing his story as I tried to rationalize it all in my mind. I wondered if Cynthia's list matched the one I found in Brock's office.

"Except she never made the meeting."

"By that time, it was too dangerous. The wheels were already in motion. Someone had tried to kill her on more than one occasion. After the latest failed attempt, I couldn't risk someone following through. So we faked her death and she relocated somewhere safe, somewhere no one will find her...somewhere *I* won't even be able to find her."

I stepped back, pulling my bottom lip between my teeth as I studied him. Something about his story just didn't sit right with me. It seemed a little too convenient that Cynthia, who the world thought killed herself before going to her arranged meeting with Dante, was now suddenly alive, but he didn't want anyone to know and offered no actual proof that she was. If I hadn't been around his lies most of my life, maybe I would believe him. But I couldn't, particularly with the knowledge that *he* sent Cynthia the threatening email. That was the one piece in this puzzle that just didn't fit, the one piece that threw his story off.

"I know what you're thinking, Ellie," he said, cutting through my thoughts. "I'm not the one behind this. I want answers just as much as Cynthia, Dante...you. I couldn't stomach the idea of anything happening to Cynthia because of..." He trailed off, taking a deep breath to compose himself. If I hadn't seen him pull the same move during funerals for fallen soldiers, I would have thought it was authentic. Too bad I knew better.

"Why don't you just go to the authorities?" I hardened my stare, not allowing his caring tone to soften my determination. "And what's to stop me from doing so if you won't?"

"Absolutely nothing," he answered with a defeated sigh. "If that's what you think you should do, I can't stop you. I can only beg and plead with you not to. By doing so, you'll put over a dozen lives at risk...including your own and Dante's."

"It's a bit suspicious, isn't it? You know how much I care for him, so you want me to think his life could be in jeopardy if I do something to bring any attention to whatever this is."

He tilted his head, the stoic politician returning. It was obvious he was becoming more and more frustrated with my questions the longer we spoke. "I'm not quite sure gambling with a person's life is the way for you to learn I'm speaking the truth, but if you'd like to see for yourself, be my guest. Just don't say I didn't warn you. It's a miracle he wasn't killed when he showed up for his meeting with Cynthia. I'm still not sure why, considering these people had to know he looking into this."

I glared at him, my eyes unwavering, an internal tug-of-war waging inside as to what story to believe. When I overheard Dante's conversation that day in Italy, I was convinced my father was involved. It made sense then. Now I wasn't sure about anything. This man was my father. Despite everything, there was this small part of me that wanted to think he wouldn't be involved in something so manipulative and devious. But if he wasn't, why would he send those emails to Cynthia, threatening her to put an end to the "Dante Luciano problem", as he referred to it? Until I could figure out which story to believe, I needed to remain guarded. It was the only option.

"Why wouldn't she just come forward with what she knew?"

"The same reason she allowed herself to be blackmailed in the first place. She's worried for the safety of her loved ones. She needs to stay hidden and alive so when we figure out who's behind all of this, we can bring them down. Until then, it's important she remain in hiding."

"You have to realize how absurd this sounds."

"Ellie…" He placed his hands on my biceps, his eyes

sincere. It was a new look for him. "I know I haven't exactly been the best father to you. I put my career first when I should have been putting you first. It was the only thing that…" He trailed off, as if recalling painful, yet happy memories.

"The only thing that what?" I pressed.

He snapped back to the present. "It doesn't matter. I'll never get that time back. But I *can* do everything in my power to make things right going forward. And that's exactly what I plan on doing from here on out. That will have to be enough reassurance for you for now."

Before I could argue with him any further, he wrapped his arms around me, taking me by complete surprise. I couldn't remember the last time my father hugged me when there weren't cameras. It was probably before I entered adolescence, when he was full of so much life and zeal…before public office took its toll on him. I wished I could melt into his arms and have the father-daughter relationship I always dreamed of and wanted. I still had too many unanswered questions. My father had always been able to spin a good story. For all I knew, he just told me a whopper of a tale. This man had already fooled me once. I wasn't going to let him do it again.

CHAPTER TEN

I STARED AT MY computer screen in my office, the setting sun beaming into the space around me. Several weeks had passed since I'd eavesdropped on my father's conversation in a dive bar down the street. Several weeks where I'd used the mediocre investigative skills I possessed to try and figure out which way was up. Several weeks where I was no closer to finding out what happened than I was back in Italy.

A slight knock tore me out of my thoughts. I glanced up to see Blake, the law firm's investigator, pop his head into my office. "Just wanted to make sure you didn't have any questions about the report I sent you earlier on the Lawrence fraud case."

I met his eyes, giving him a smile. He was a younger guy. Most investigators I'd worked with in the past had been cops who retired after twenty years, but still missed the job. Blake was just a few years older than me. He joined the army straight out of high school, eventually becoming a CID special agent before deciding to take the plunge back into civilian life.

"It's perfect. Everything I could have needed, and then some."

"That's what I like to hear." He paused, his green eyes beaming with pride. "Well, I'm off. See you

Monday, Elle. Have a great weekend."

"You, too," I replied, returning my eyes to my computer as he headed down the hall. "Blake, wait!"

He popped his head back into my office. "Yeah?"

Chewing on my bottom lip, I stared at him, torn. I knew once I put the wheels into motion, there would be no going back, but I'd gotten nowhere trying to get answers on my own. Maybe I needed a fresh set of eyes, an unbiased set of eyes…a highly trained, investigative set of eyes. Yes, Steven was an FBI agent, but that was precisely why I couldn't involve him in this. I needed someone who could help me discreetly without opening a federal investigation.

"Can you close the door?"

He studied me, but his curiosity eventually got the better of him. He closed the door, then took a seat in one of the chairs on the opposite side of my desk. "What's up?"

"There's been something that's been bothering me, something I've been looking into, but haven't been able to find out much. I just… I'd like your help, but I need a bit of discretion on your part."

"Help I can give you, but discretion can only go so far. If I find out information that can prevent the commission of a crime—"

I held up a hand. "I understand completely. But until that point, I'd ask that this conversation, as well as anything you uncover, stay between us."

After considering my request for a moment, he nodded. "I can do that."

Taking a deep breath, I opened the top drawer of my desk and pulled out a copy of the file I'd amassed over the past several weeks. "I want you to look into my father." I pushed the folder across the desk to him.

He lifted a brow. "Your father?"

I'd only been working here a little more than a month, but I'd become somewhat close to Blake, thanks to Quinn's insistence I go to Happy Hour with the rest of the staff every week. Throughout the course of our conversations, I'd revealed who I was... Eleanor Crenshaw. The one who ditched her politician fiancé at the altar. The one whose father was Francis Crenshaw, a senior member of the Senate. The one whose affair with a famous Italian chef briefly made headlines.

"Yes." I straightened my spine. "And his connection to a woman named Cynthia Edelman. She supposedly committed suicide back in March, but..." I shrugged.

"But you don't think that was the case."

"I don't know what to think," I admitted. "I've never had the best relationship with my father, with either of my parents, so I think my animosity may be clouding my judgment. I need someone who is completely detached to look into this and see what they can find."

He opened his mouth, hesitating, and I sensed he was about to refuse to help. He was my last hope at getting answers. I needed him to agree.

"I can pay you," I blurted out before he could utter a single syllable. "Probably not much, but I'll—"

"Elle..." He reached out and placed his hand over mine. "I want to help you, but there's no turning back after this. If I find out something, if I know there's criminal activity and have the evidence to back it up…"

"I know." I gave him a small smile.

Why was this so difficult? I wasn't exactly close to my father. I didn't know how I was supposed to feel about him not being the man I thought he was when I was younger, when I idolized him, when he was my hero. This would eat me up until I could get some concrete answers, regardless of what those answers were.

"I need to know, no matter what."

He blew out a long breath, pulling his hand away. "Okay."

"All the information I've been able to find out is in that file. There's a list of drugs I'd like you to see what you can find out about, questionable deaths, stuff like that. I'd also like you to look into any suspicious incidents around the vicinity of Barnes Pharmaceuticals in the weeks leading up to Cynthia Edelman's death."

"Why?"

"It might help. That's all. Then again, it could be nothing, but please, just humor me."

He nodded and grabbed the file, standing.

"Thank you, Blake," I said sincerely. "You have my cell number in case anything comes up over the weekend?"

"I'm sure that won't be necessary. Something like this will probably take some time, especially considering you don't want to raise any suspicions. Even if I do find anything over the next few days, it can wait until

Monday."

"Probably. But in case it can't, you know how to reach me."

"I do." He paused, his mouth curving into a small smile. "Have a nice weekend."

"You, too."

As soon as he disappeared down the hall, I sank back into my chair, blowing out the breath I'd been holding. Would I come to regret involving Blake in this? Probably, but I didn't know what else to do. This seemed to be my only option.

Returning my attention to my monitor, I eyed the time in the upper right-hand corner, immediately jumping to my feet. I hastily shut down my computer, collected all my papers, and shoved them into my bag. Within a few seconds, I hurried out of the office and was on my way to a bar down the street to meet Mila for a few drinks.

Once I moved out of her house, it had become part of our routine to get together before I headed to my mother's weekly dinner party. And I still went, if for no other reason than to have a few minutes alone with my father to try and get more answers out of him, to let out a little more rope to see if he hung himself. But, regardless of my prodding, he stuck to his story, not offering so much of a hint as to where Cynthia Edelman could be or this supposed secret she had been blackmailed over.

Rushing through the front doors of the upscale wine bar, I spied Mila sitting on one of the stools, enjoying a glass of what appeared to be a freshly poured red wine.

"Sorry I'm late." I took the seat beside her. "I lost track of time."

"It's okay," she replied, sipping from her glass. "I just got here myself. Traffic was a bit rough. You'd think it wouldn't be, considering I was going against rush hour."

"That's LA for you." I raised my hand, flagging down the bartender and placing my order. "There's no such thing as no traffic."

"Ain't that the truth. I'm glad I'm a stay-at-home Mom. I couldn't imagine sitting in traffic for two hours just to go thirty miles. I'd lose my shit after ten minutes."

"Audiobooks are a lifesaver," I offered. "But it's not so bad now that I live so close to work. I barely spend any time in my car these days."

"Which is probably a good thing," Mila joked. "I told you to just keep Steven's car while you saved money for something better."

I smiled at the bartender when he placed my wine in front of me. "I know. And I appreciate the offer, but I have a job. I need to start making my own way. And my car isn't *that* bad. Is it old? Yes. But I've yet to have a single problem with it." I tapped on the top of the bar. "Knock on wood."

"Because you barely drive anywhere. Just promise you'll think about getting something a little better when you have the money."

I gave her a smile. "Of course."

"Good." She took a sip of her drink before straightening her back. "So…" Her voice brightened. "What was today's love letter?"

My mood immediately lifted. I'd been so preoccupied with my father lately that the only ray of light, the only things that made me smile, were the Instagram posts from Dante. And he still sent at least one a day, no matter where he was or what he was doing.

I grabbed my phone and found his most recent post, handing it to Mila. She studied my phone for several seconds, then read the caption out loud.

"'We are much fonder of the pictures of those we love when they are at a great distance than when they are near to us.' - Hèloïse d'Argenteuil, *Letters of Abelard and Hèloïse.*"

"It's the grave of Hèloïse and Abelard at Père Lachaise Cemetery in Paris," I explained. "It must be an older photo, since he's not in Paris right now." I looked straight ahead, avoiding her eyes.

"Speaking of which—"

"Do you know the story of Hèloïse and Abelard?" I interrupted, not wanting her to ask the next question. I knew all too well what that would be.

She looked at me, subtly shaking her head.

"It was a tragic story, one with no happy ending. It was a forbidden romance before that became the trendy thing. She was estimated to be twenty-two years his junior…and his student. Regardless, that didn't stop them from falling in love and eventually having a baby, as the legend goes. When Hèloïse's uncle found out, he wasn't happy. To keep her safe, Abelard placed her in a convent. Her uncle thought it was Abelard's way of getting rid of her so he had Abelard castrated. Despite the obstacles, the two sent letters to each other throughout the years." I sighed, a dreamy expression crossing my face as I allowed myself to be filled with hope, regardless of how ill-placed it was. "Their love never wavered, even until Abelard's dying day."

It was silent for a moment as I considered whether that was all I had to look forward to — a daily Instagram post, a distant love that would go on for years.

"That's beautiful, Ellie," Mila remarked, snapping me out of my thoughts.

I brought my wine to my lips, savoring the spiciness of the pinot, then lowered the glass back to the bar. "Now the letters are nearly as famous as the affair itself. People flock to their grave in Paris, hoping to surround themselves with just a fraction of the love they had."

"What did you send back to Dante?"

I grabbed my phone again, bringing up the photo I'd found online of a closeup of a coin on the ledge of the Trevi Fountain. It was the only thing that seemed fitting. I always returned to the fountain. I had a feeling I always would. It was where I left my heart.

I passed my cell to Mila and she read the caption out loud.

"'For not with me was my heart, but with thee. But now, more than ever, if it be not with thee, it is nowhere. For without thee it cannot anywhere exist.' -

127

T.K. Leigh

Hèloïse d'Argenteuil, *Letters of Abelard and Hèloïse.*"

She handed my phone back to me, pausing for a moment. "It's fitting, isn't it? You two are like a modern day Hèloïse and Abelard. The love letters are just in the form of Instagram posts. It's one of those stories you'll be able to tell your kids one day. I bet yours are going be absolutely adorable. Much better than what your kids with Brock would have looked like." She cringed in playful disgust. "Not because of you. You're beautiful. And Brock's a decent-looking guy, but I'm convinced there's something off about him."

I swallowed hard, avoiding her eyes. I still hadn't seen Brock in a while, which had begun to unnerve me, especially since he'd flown halfway around the world to track me down. I couldn't quite explain it, but something about his lack of contact didn't sit right with me. I wondered if he knew what I found in his office back in June. More pressing was *why* he had all that stuff. It looked like he was investigating my father. It was possible, but I couldn't shake the feeling that Brock's involvement went beyond that. He and my father had routinely worked together to get certain bills passed in both the House and Senate. I wondered if their relationship went beyond the halls of Congress.

"It's kind of difficult to make babies when we live thousands of miles away from each other."

Mila opened her mouth to respond, but I quickly cut her off, knowing exactly what she was about to say.

"Maybe we're just doomed to be apart until we're old and gray. Then they'll find our Instagram posts and

128

publish them. They'll bury our bodies together, and people will flock to our graves, just like Hèloïse and Abelard."

"I don't understand why you haven't gone to him," she stated in a quiet voice.

I kept my eyes trained forward, trying to pretend I didn't know what she was referring to as I signaled the bartender for another glass of wine. "I haven't exactly been able to afford a trip to Rome, Mila. I'm finally making my own way, but after rent, utilities, and chipping away at the credit card balance I racked up during my months of unemployment, not to mention the expense of my previous trip to the Eternal City, there's not much left over."

"That's not what I mean. Even it if were, I told you I'd let you borrow—"

"No," I shot back immediately, my voice rising in pitch as I glowered at her. Then I softened my expression, bringing my fresh wine to my lips and taking a sip. "I'm sorry. I appreciate everything you've done for me. I truly do. But it's important that I stand on my own two feet."

"Which you've proven you can do. You have a job. An apartment. A...car, I suppose," she said, grimacing. "Although car is putting it loosely."

I laughed politely at her jab. I doubted I'd ever hear the end of it. It wasn't a bad car, but it certainly wasn't even close to the luxury vehicles I'd driven since getting my license.

"It's okay to ask for help when you need it, to accept

it when it's freely given."

I vehemently shook my head. "No. Not me. I just… I can't. I need to do this on my own so I can figure out who I am."

"Says who?" she shot back quickly. "You think you need to suffer and be unhappy just to figure out who you are?"

"Yes!" I insisted, tears welling in my eyes. I drew in a deep breath, meeting her concerned gaze. "That's got to be what this is all about, why we're still apart. I thought once I had a job and a place of my own, we'd find each other again. Maybe that's what fate's waiting for before we can be together."

She placed her hand over mine, squeezing. "I love you, Ellie, but you need to stop depriving yourself of being happy because of some idea you have in your head that you don't know who you are as a person. I'll tell you a secret. *I'm* still trying to figure that out for myself. You don't just wake up one day and miraculously have your shit together. Life doesn't work that way. Life is a path we take, with ebbs and flows, ups and downs. It's better when you can take that path with someone who supports you, who loves you, who makes you a better person."

"It's not that easy. Not for me."

"I get it, Ellie. Your mother ingrained this notion into your head that being happy makes you selfish. Well, fuck that and fuck her." She lowered her voice. "You still love him, so why are you punishing yourself like this? Why are you having a drink with me, then planning to go to your parents' house when you know damn well you should be somewhere else?"

My eyes narrowed at her, my lips formed into a tight line. "I told you—"

"I know. What's meant to be will be," she bit back in a mocking tone. "Did you ever stop to think maybe you're doing everything in your power to work *against* fate? Dante is in town for a particular award show this weekend. I know he also has an appearance scheduled at USC tonight. And I know *you* know that, too." She raised her glass of wine to her lips, leaning back in her chair, a satisfied smile on her face. "Sometimes, my darling friend, fate needs a little push."

CHAPTER ELEVEN

MILA'S WORDS SEEMED TO play on repeat in my mind as I headed up the walkway toward my parents' house. About to knock on the front door, I hesitated, glancing back at my car, wondering if she was right, if maybe fate needed a little push, if I'd simply been depriving myself of being happy. Before I had the chance to leave, the door flew open, my mother standing there.

"What is *that?*" she asked, a look of disgust on her face as she gestured to the car sitting in her driveway. I was certain she was horrified enough when I'd been driving Steven's car, considering it was a Ford and not some luxury brand. Now that I was driving a Subaru that was over ten years old, it was even worse.

"It's my new car," I replied with a passive-aggressive smile. "Do you like it? Got a great deal on it. I bought it over a month ago. I'm surprised you're now just noticing."

"I've been too busy with all my charity work to concern myself with what car you're driving, Ellie."

I rolled my eyes, fighting back a sarcastic retort at the notion of my mother doing anything for charity.

"I do hope *they* paid *you* to take it off their hands, not the other way around," she continued when I remained silent.

"No, Mother. *I* paid for it." I pushed past her and stepped into the house, then spun around to face her. "With money from a job I got on my merits."

"Oh, really?" She lifted a brow. "You think that's the case?"

My expression faltered briefly. While it had crossed my mind that Quinn may have hired me just to say he had the daughter of a political powerhouse working at his small firm in order to increase his credibility, I wanted to think he wasn't so shallow, that he brought me on because of my talent and tenacity to fight for my clients. I *needed* to believe that was why he hired me.

"Yes, I do." I crossed my arms in front of my chest, holding my chin high.

She leaned into me, her lips formed in a tight line. "You can believe that all you want, but the only reason anyone would ever hire you is because of your name, Ellie. The only reason you got the job at Sullivan was because of me. And I guarantee the only reason you were hired at your current...job," she said with mild distaste, "was because of me. You'd be nothing without me. Don't you *ever* forget that." She glowered at me for a moment longer, then stepped back, plastering a fake smile on her face. "Now, let's go greet our guests. There are a few potential donors to your father's campaign present this evening. Even though he's busy, we still need to do our part and show them the mother-daughter bond they believe exists."

She headed toward the formal sitting room,

expecting me to follow her, but my feet remained rooted to the floor. It wasn't until she almost disappeared around the corner that she realized I was no longer beside her. She spun around, her fierce eyes narrowed on me, indignation covering the lines of her face. She opened her mouth, about to berate me, but I interrupted her.

"Why do you hate me so much?" I asked in a quiet voice.

"Don't be absurd," she scoffed. "I'm tired of this behavior. I've let it slide the past few months, but it's getting old. Now, come. Let's not keep our guests waiting."

"No, Mother." I narrowed my eyes at her, remaining firmly in place.

Regardless of the amount of jabs and insults this woman had flung at me over the past twenty-eight years, I continued to do what she wanted, even after returning from Italy. I had accomplished everything on my list, apart from truly separating myself from my mother's overbearing shadow. I still showed up here every Friday night because she demanded it. Yes, I told myself the reason for my presence was to get more information out of my father, but was that really it? I knew my father wouldn't even be here tonight. He was in San Francisco to prepare for a campaign rally there tomorrow morning. The fact I still came here was the slap in the face I needed. I was still under this woman's thumb. It was time I freed myself from her hold once and for all.

"Why. Do. You. Hate. Me? Why this animosity toward me?" I simply stared at her, waiting for an answer.

She took several steps toward me, keeping her voice low so no one could overhear our conversation, not wanting anyone to think we were anything but the perfect family. "How could you even say such a thing?" Her expression softened, but I knew it was just an act. I doubted this woman had ever uttered a sincere word in her life. "I took care of you. I fed you. Bathed you. Soothed your cries when you woke up at two in the morning."

"That doesn't mean anything. If you loved me, why would you tell me there was no Santa?"

She straightened her spine, taken aback by my question, her brows furrowing. "What are you talking about?"

"You know *exactly* what I'm talking about." The vein in my forehead throbbed, my jaw tightening. "I couldn't have been more than three years old. I rushed down the stairs Christmas morning to see what Santa had brought me, only to find out he hadn't come." I stepped toward her, struggling to keep my composure, the memory of that morning still raw. I lost more than the childhood hope Santa represented. I lost the hope of having the love of a family. "When I asked you why, you told me he wasn't real. I was three. *Three*! How could you be so cruel and heartless to a little girl?"

She blinked repeatedly before straightening, her expression resolute, unwavering. "Because, Ellie. The sooner you realized how the world worked the better. Life isn't all fairy tales and dreams. It's hard. It's painful. Apparently, you still want to live up in the clouds somewhere."

"I'd rather be in the clouds and happy than down here on earth and miserable…like you." I glared at her, my hardened stare slowly softening.

Stepping back, I took stock of my surroundings. Vaulted entryway. Marble tile. Pristine floral arrangements. The sound of polite chatter coming from the sitting room. This was what my life had always consisted of. The image of perfection. Putting on an act. Not letting anyone see what hid behind the mask we all wore, disguising who we truly were. I left Italy to figure out who I was. Maybe I had known all along.

"What am I doing here?" I murmured to myself.

"You're doing what you're supposed to be doing," my mother replied in a clipped tone. "You're here to show the donors to your father's campaign that we're the picture of a happy family. It's taken a lot of convincing on my part after your little…wedding fiasco. But people are finally starting to forget about that, as evidenced by Brock finally being ahead in the polls again. So, come into the sitting room, tone down the snide comments for one night, and show these people we're the typical American family with the values they want to see in Congress, then perhaps the White House."

I backed away, slowly shaking my head. "No."

My mother stopped, taken by surprise, her wide eyes

136

narrowing at me. "No?"

"That's right."

Smiling, an excitement I hadn't felt since waiting for Dante in front of the Spanish Steps sparked in my veins. I immediately knew the path I was supposed to be on, and this was not it. Mila was right. Sometimes fate *did* need a push.

"I have to go." I spun around, heading toward the door.

"Where do you think you're going?" my mother demanded, stalking after me.

"Back to the clouds," I replied, rushing out of the house.

CHAPTER TWELVE

I TAPPED MY FINGERNAILS on the steering wheel, glancing at the clock, then the GPS on my phone. It was currently 8:45 PM. Dante's appearance at USC ended at ten. The GPS indicated I would get there at 10:04. All I could do was hope to catch him in time. I almost expected my car to be dead when I tried to start it up after running out of my parents' house. Instead, it whirred to life, making me think perhaps fate was looking out for me after all. When I merged onto the freeway, I was somewhat surprised I wasn't immediately met with red brake lights. Of course, that surprise was short-lived. Within a few miles, the notorious traffic on the 101 came to a slow crawl, then almost a dead stop.

"Are you trying to tell me something?" I muttered under my breath, feeling the engine sputter a bit. "No, girl. You've got this." I rubbed the dashboard. "Don't give out on me now. Please. Just let me get to Dante, then you can keel over and die a spectacular death, but not now."

The car made a few more noises, then miraculously evened out. I released a relieved breath as I tilted my head back, looking through the sunroof at the stars above me.

"Please, God," I began. "I know we haven't exactly

been on a first-name basis most of my life, but if you could just find it in your heart to help me tonight, I promise I'll never take your name in vain or violate any of those other amendments or commandments or whatever you call them. I'll even try to go to church more than once a decade. Just let me get to him. Okay?"

I chewed on my bottom lip, as if waiting for someone to answer. When a horn blared, I snapped my eyes forward, seeing that the car in front of me had moved several yards. I stepped on the gas, inching along the freeway.

Nearly the entire way there, traffic was at a crawl. It picked up a little here and there, getting my hopes up, only to come to a standstill again. I always loved living in Southern California, but right now, I cursed the traffic that plagued this city.

As I slowly made my way closer to USC, I couldn't take the freeway congestion anymore, my nerves and anxiety at an all-time high. I was so close, but the GPS now showed I wouldn't get there until 10:15. I couldn't risk it. I swerved onto the shoulder, zooming by all the cars honking at me as I passed, then took one of the exits for downtown LA. The instant I merged onto the city streets, my shoulders relaxed, relieved I was finally able to go faster than five miles an hour. I glanced at my clock again. 9:51. I almost wanted to pick up my phone and tag Dante in an Instagram post to tell him I was on my way. With my luck, though, fate would make sure a cop saw me, who would then pull me over for texting and driving. I didn't want to tempt fate any more than I already was.

Just as I passed all the congestion that typically surrounded the Staples Center and thought I was in the clear, I slammed on the brakes, police barricades blocking anyone from driving any farther on Figueroa.

"You've *got* to be kidding me!" I screamed, gripping the steering wheel, my nostrils flaring. Anxious, I glanced at the clock on my dashboard again. 9:58. I craned my neck to determine how far the backup of cars went as a result of the detour. All I saw were red brake lights for several blocks, if not more. Refusing to let fate push back, I scanned the street for a parking spot. Of course, there weren't any.

My car inched along, the tension in my body building. For every minute that ticked by, my hope this would be the night our separation ended faded even more. Maybe it was too soon. Maybe it wasn't the right time. Maybe I still had unfinished business to take care of before we could be together. But I wasn't willing to give up. Not yet. Not now.

After an excruciatingly long time, my patience non-existent, I finally reached a side street and was able to veer away from the traffic, taking a left, then a right, returning to Figueroa. It seemed a little too easy. I expected something else to happen to prevent me from getting to USC. Instead, the campus appeared in front of me, the brick pillars holding the sign a welcome sight. I checked the time again. 10:12. I couldn't waste a second looking around for a spot in one of the parking garages on campus. Instead, I pulled into a no parking zone on the street. At this point, I didn't care if my car ended up being towed. The only thing I cared about was getting to Dante before he slipped from my grasp.

Grabbing my purse, I jumped out of my car and hurried toward campus, unsure of where his appearance was being held. Even if I knew what building, I wouldn't have any clue where to find it. I'd never been here before. The way my luck had been going tonight, I was probably on the opposite end of campus from where I needed to be.

Walking at a quick pace, I pulled my phone from my purse, consulting Google to see if I could find out where he would be. Not looking where I was going, the heel of my shoe got stuck in a crack in the sidewalk and my ankle twisted.

"Dammit!" I exclaimed, gritting my teeth through the pain. After taking a moment, I yanked off my shoes, then continued limping through campus, doing my best not to pay any attention to the shooting ache radiating through my ankle. A voice in my head told me this was yet another sign it was too soon, that I should just forget about it. If this wasn't fate telling me to back off, I didn't know what it was. But I wasn't going to let her win. Not when I was so close that I could almost see his smile. I could almost taste his lips. I could almost smell his aroma.

As I trekked through campus, I spied an advertisement taped to a lamppost, Dante's brilliant smile beaming back at me. I hurried to the poster, reading it out loud. "Eight to ten PM. World-famous chef and journalist Dante Luciano. Bovard Auditorium."

With absolutely no idea where that was, I spun in a circle, looking at the names of the buildings encircling me in the quad. A beehive of activity surrounded the steps of one of them, so I limped toward it. This had to be the place. There was no other reason for a building on a college campus to be so busy on a Friday night.

Approaching the front steps, I overheard several discussions about what country they'd want to visit most if money were no object, and knew I was in the right spot. I raced up the steps, pushing my way against the current of people coming out of the building, praying Dante was still here. I squeezed into the lobby and checked my watch. 10:22 PM.

"Please, God," I murmured as I hurried toward a set of doors leading into the theater. "Let him be here." I reached for the handle, but an usher prevented me from going any farther.

"I apologize, ma'am. No re-admittance. Did you leave something? If you tell me where you were sitting and what it was, I can have one of our ushers look for it."

"I didn't leave anything. I...," I stammered, hoping I wouldn't come off sounding like an obsessed fan. "I came to see Dante."

"You and over a thousand other people."

"I know. I just... Is he still here?"

"No, ma'am," he said in a drawn-out voice, looking me up and down. It was readily apparent that he thought I was crazy. And I probably looked it — out of breath, hair disheveled, barefoot, holding a pair of heels, limping. "You're about twenty minutes too late."

My shoulders fell. I briefly closed my eyes, releasing a heavy sigh. Maybe Mila was wrong. Maybe fate didn't need a little push. Because I pushed, but fate seemed to do everything in her power to stand in my way.

"Isn't that the story of my life?" I remarked as I shuffled away, my voice barely audible from the frustration building in my throat, in my heart.

I emerged into the crisp night air, my body chilled now that the adrenaline had worn off. Holding onto the railing, I carefully stepped down the short set of stairs, keeping my eyes downturned as I made my way through the thinning crowd outside the theater. Jealousy bubbled inside me at the notion that all these people had been in Dante's presence this evening, had heard his voice, had seen his smile. They didn't realize how lucky they were.

Pausing for a moment, I glanced back at the building, considering whether or not I should take a photo of myself in front of it and tag Dante so he knew I tried to get to him. In the end, I resisted the urge. Maybe it was better this way. Maybe we *were* doomed to the same fate of Hèloïse and Abelard. Maybe our love was best shared in love letters…or, in our case, Instagram posts.

With slow steps, I limped through campus, my ankle now screaming at me. A few people, clearly students, stopped to ask if I needed any help, but I refused their assistance. I didn't mind the pain. It was nothing compared to the ache in my heart, my frustration turning into despair. I'd done everything to stay mostly positive through our separation, thinking fate would eventually bring us together again. I didn't know how much longer I could do that.

When I finally reached the street where I parked, my car nowhere to be found, all I could do was laugh hysterically.

"I get it!" I shouted to the sky. "You win, okay?" I was certain I looked like a complete lunatic — standing on the dirty sidewalk in downtown Los Angeles, holding a pair of heels, my hair disheveled and dress askew from all the running I'd done. "I give up." I shook my head, doing my best to stop my chin from quivering, barely able to speak through the painful lump in my throat. "I give up."

I didn't know why I thought this would work, that I'd get to him, that he'd see me and immediately sweep me into his arms, begging me in his husky, commanding voice to never leave him again. The image in my head was so real. I could almost hear his voice and feel his arms around me. Why couldn't *that* be my reality?

Defeated, I reached into my purse and grabbed my phone, about to call for an Uber, but paused. I didn't want to go home and be reminded of how miserable I was. To see all the clothes Dante had bought me hanging in my sad excuse for a closet. To lay awake in an empty bed, the memory of falling asleep beside him gutting me. I just needed a moment to myself, then I could move on. It was time I finally moved on.

Tears prickling my eyes, I limped down the street, crossed the train tracks, and headed toward what had become one of my favorite spots during my unemployment — the Rose Garden by the Colosseum. The instant I walked through the archway, a sort of tranquility washed over me, the hustle of Los Angeles all but vanishing. I hoped the peacefulness could quiet the troubled thoughts invading my subconscious, help me stop feeling, make me numb, even if for just a minute.

I walked past rows of perfectly manicured rose bushes, the bulbs in full bloom. I took my time as I made my way up the path toward the fountain in the center, stopping to smell a few of the roses, the powdery sweet aroma calming me like a baby's blanket.

I drew closer to the fountain, smiling wistfully at the sight of a couple who had obviously just come from their wedding reception and were having their photos taken. I gazed upon them with a mixture of envy and longing. They looked so happy, so in love. I experienced that for a brief moment, but was stubborn and pushed it away. And for what?

My ankle throbbing, I took a moment to rest on a bench in front of the fountain. As I watched the water dance in the sky before falling back into the pool, I couldn't help but think of Dante. Everything seemed to remind me of him. Fountains. Coffee. Pasta. Wine. Even things as simple as an old tree and fresh-cut grass. It only took a week, but he'd ingrained himself in every facet of my life. So much so that even three months later, my need for him had only grown stronger, the hole in my heart where his love used to be leaving me empty.

I closed my eyes, imagining that we were back in Italy in front of the Trevi Fountain. But this time, instead of me saying I needed to leave, I agreed to stay. The smile and relief that washed over his expression when I finally gave him what he wanted, what *I* wanted, made my heart nearly burst. I ran my fingers over my lips, almost able to feel his mouth on mine, the scruff of his two-day beard scratching my skin.

I wrapped my arms around my body, fighting back the tears forming in my eyes. His intoxicating aroma of basil, mint, and licorice seemed to grow stronger with each breath I took, as if his scent were permanently ingrained in my nostrils. I wondered if I would always smell it, even after years. Even after we both moved on with our lives and tried to find that same happiness we'd been lucky enough to experience for too short a time. Even when we turned to dust.

My phone chimed, snapping me out of my fantasy world. I looked at where it sat on my lap. When I saw I'd been tagged in one of Dante's posts, I inhaled a shaky breath at the irony. Biting my lips to stop my chin from quivering, I wiped at my tears, doing my best to reel in my emotions, despite the constant lump in my throat becoming more pronounced with each passing second. I didn't know if I could bear to look at his post. Not anymore. Not knowing fate obviously didn't think we belonged together. But I'd become addicted to these posts from him, had grown dependent on his words for my own happiness.

Maybe tonight was fate's way of telling me it was time I found something else that made me happy.

"Just one more," I said to myself. "Then I'll stop. It's time to stop."

Picking up my phone with a shaky hand, I reluctantly opened the Instagram app, clicking on Dante's most recent post. My eyes fell on the image and I quickly shot off the bench, paying no attention to my ankle. I turned around in a circle, looking everywhere for a familiar face, but the only people I saw were the newlyweds and their wedding photographer.

I looked back at my phone, staring at the photo of me sitting in this exact spot, my back facing the camera, wearing the dress I currently had on, my hair styled the same, right down to the tangled mess of its present state. I glanced up again, scanning the area, the world seeming to spin around me. He was here. I could feel it. In my veins. In my bones. In my heart.

"Where are you?" I murmured, limping around the fountain as I frantically searched for him, my chest heaving. If he wasn't here, if this was just a cruel joke, I didn't know how I would survive. I was ready to fall apart as it was. This… This would wreck me.

I returned my eyes to my phone to determine the exact angle he'd snapped the photo. When I finally noticed the caption, I stopped moving, allowing the words to wash over me. Instantly, I sensed a warmth approach from behind, just like that day back in June when I waited for him in front of the Spanish Steps.

Then it hit me. That voice I'd dreamt about. The heat I'd longed to feel on my skin. "'I'll follow thee and make a heaven of hell, to die upon the hand I love so well.' William Shakespeare. *A Midsummer Night's Dream.*"

God, it sounded so real, right down to his toe-curling accent. I wanted to believe it was, but what if it wasn't? What if I finally hit my breaking point?

"Please tell me this isn't a joke," I begged in a shaky tone, refusing to turn around, worried I'd do so and find myself alone.

"It's not a joke, Eleanor." A hand fell on my hip, forcing me around.

I stared into his dark eyes and reached for his face, choking out a sob when I felt the scruff against my trembling hand. I drew my body closer as he cupped my cheeks, both of us gazing at each other, worried we'd blink and it would all disappear.

"How are you here?" I whispered.

"I was about to ask you the same question." He wiped the tears cascading down my face, his eyes wet with unshed tears of his own.

"I pushed fate and she pushed back," I explained, swallowing hard. "I tried to get to you, but everything that could go wrong did. I thought it was fate telling me it wasn't meant to be."

He brought his body even closer, lowering his mouth toward mine. Our breath intermingled, his eyes searing me, the fire that had grown dull over the past few months now a raging inferno once more.

"And now?"

"Now I can't help but think that fate has a terrible sense of humor." I laughed slightly, another tear trickling down my cheek. Swiping at it, his thumb traveled across my face and caressed my bottom lip, sending a spark through me.

"Tell me, Eleanor," he began, hope building in his gaze. "Have you had enough time to figure out who you are?"

My eyes locked on his, I gave him the only answer I could. "I don't know who I am without you. You're a part of me. Without you in my life, I'm hopelessly incomplete."

He smiled, exhaling a short breath. His lips ghosted against mine, giving me the slightest hint of a kiss. "It took you long enough to figure that out." He pressed his hand to my back, erasing the last bit of distance between us. Then he kissed me, fully, beautifully, completely, the feeling of his lips on mine releasing all the tension that had built up over our months of separation.

I moaned, running my fingers through his hair as I deepened the exchange, telling him without words how much I missed him, how much I needed him, how much I loved him. Our kiss was passionate, greedy, and perfect in all the ways I imagined it would be.

He pulled away. "Eleanor," he panted, cupping my face, his gaze intense.

"Yes?" I swallowed hard.

"Don't ever make me live without you again. Please. I just... It makes no sense, but I don't ever want to be the person I am without you. Okay?"

I smiled through my tears. "I don't ever want to be

the person I am without you, either. You found me, just like I hoped you would. Now you're stuck with me."

"*Sempre e per sempre?*" He lifted a brow as his lips lowered to mine once more.

"*Sempre e per sempre.* Always and forever."

As his tongue swept against mine, his arms holding me in a way that made me think he'd never let go, his need consumed me. I finally lowered the walls I'd constructed over the previous twenty-eight years of my life. I finally realized I was worthy of everything I'd been deprived of before. Happiness. Devotion. *Love.*

This time, I wasn't going to let it go without a fight.

CHAPTER THIRTEEN

I STRUGGLED TO KEEP up with Dante's long strides as he pulled me through the elaborate lobby of the Beverly Wilshire, my heels sliding on the slick, shiny tile. He slowed his steps, glancing back at me.

"Are you limping?" He lifted a brow.

I faltered briefly before correcting myself. While we made our way from the Rose Garden and into an Uber, I'd been conscious to act as if I weren't in any pain. I'd almost forgotten about my ankle…until now.

"My heel got caught in a crack in the sidewalk when I was trying to get to you before your appearance was over." I tried to play it off as I continued toward the elevators, tugging him along with me. "I twisted my ankle or something."

He immediately came to a stop, forcing me to stop, as well. "Why didn't you say anything?" His eyes raked over every inch of me. His obvious concern for my well-being warmed my heart, reminding me why I'd fallen for him so hard, so fast, so easily. "We need to get you to a doctor."

"No, we don't." Vehemently shaking my head, I raised myself onto my toes, doing my best to hide any sign of discomfort. The last thing I needed was to sit in a waiting room for hours just for a doctor to tell me to put some ice on it. There was only one thing I needed at this moment, only one thing that could heal the pain I'd been enduring the past three months, maybe longer. "I just need you, Dante."

"But—"

I pressed my lips to his, interrupting him from any further argument. As I curved my body into his, brushing against his growing erection, he groaned, any hint of his previous protest melting away. He palmed my back, the distance between us becoming non-existent. Intensifying the kiss, he breathed into me, giving me everything I'd dreamt about since I walked away from him at the airport in Rome. As the world seemed to disappear around us, I ran my hands through his thick hair. The instant his coarse locks hit my fingertips, I whimpered. I didn't think I'd ever feel his hair in my hands again, his body against mine, his lips on mine. I didn't want this moment to end. I didn't want *us* to end.

I loved this man. I was a fool to leave him once. I thought I needed to be on my own to figure out who I was, ignoring the truth that had been glaring at me like the brightest star in the sky. I already knew who I was. A woman who would do anything for love. Who would fight LA traffic. Who would disregard the rules and park in a tow zone. Who would put her safety at risk and run in heels just to chase that unmatched high one feels when in love with another human.

Gone was the woman who always did what was expected of her, who never stood up for what she wanted, who always put everyone else before her.

When I met Dante, that side of me died. I opened my mind and tried things I never thought I would. Dante had said he would show me who I was, who I was meant to be. I finally realized he had fulfilled his promise. I knew who I was. Maybe fate was waiting for me to finally figure it out.

I slowly pulled my lips away, smiling up at Dante, studying everything about him. The slight wrinkles around his eyes. The small vein in his forehead. The tanned skin. The little bit of gray hair visible in his short sideburns. The flecks of gold in his dark eyes.

"What is it?" he asked, licking his lips.

I opened my mouth slightly, completely overwhelmed, everything I'd been through the past several months washing over me — struggling to find a job, trying to figure out what my father was involved in, my mother's obvious animosity toward me. But every tear, every moment of despair, every lonesome thought... It was all worth it. To be here, to be with this man, to feel something I didn't think existed...to feel *loved*.

"You..." I shook my head, running my hand against his cheek. He melted into me, briefly closing his eyes. "I didn't..." I trailed off, struggling to come up with the words I needed. I laughed slightly. "You're the best part of me, Dante."

"It's about time you figured that out." He touched his lips to mine, treating me to a tender, warm, affectionate kiss before slowly pulling back, gazing at me with the same mixture of ardor and hunger I'd come to expect from him, reminding me of his duplicitous nature and how much I craved it, needed it, yearned for it.

Before I knew what was happening, Dante swooped me into his arms.

"What are you doing?" I shrieked, laughing as he carried me through the lobby. His smile was wide, carefree. Other hotel guests stared at us, some whispering under their breath about the scene we were making, but neither one of us cared. Dante always had an uncanny ability to make me forget about the world around us, to make me see only him. And from this moment forward, that was all I wanted. Just to see him. To never look away again.

"Three months is a very long time for a man to go without feeling your legs wrapped around him," he whispered, his tone seductive as his teeth scraped my earlobe.

"Is that right?" I shot him a coy look.

"That's right, Eleanor."

When we approached the bank of elevators, he gingerly lowered me to my feet, his eyes filled with desire as he stalked toward me. My back hit the wall and he reached past me to press the call button, his proximity and the way he seemed to leer at me like a man who hadn't seen a woman in months causing my heart rate to skyrocket. I feared the second he'd touch me, I'd shatter into a million pieces and never find them all to put myself back together again.

"Do you have any idea how much I've looked forward to this?" he murmured against my neck, his breath hot on my skin.

Goosebumps prickled my flesh, a shiver rolling through me. I knew if the wall wasn't supporting me, my legs would have given out, his sensuality, his words, his essence turning me into putty.

"To feel you shake beneath me." He pressed his body against mine, his erection prominent against my stomach. "To watch your expression as I drive harder and harder, pushing you to your breaking point." He gripped my hair, tugging it, yanking my head back as he ran his mouth over the exposed flesh of my neck. "To hear your breathing grow more ragged and uneven as you struggle not to fall apart too soon." His hand floated to my backside and he cupped my ass, causing me to yelp in surprise.

I returned my gaze to him, watching as he stepped back, his dark eyes searing my skin. My lips parting, I attempted to say something, anything. Just as Dante had done during our very first meeting, he'd rendered me completely speechless. I had a feeling he always would.

"Why did I ever walk away from you?" I mused in a low voice.

"It was what fate wanted," he answered without a moment's hesitation. "Like you said, if you didn't walk away, we never would have come down from the clouds."

"Maybe we weren't meant to. Maybe we belong in the clouds. Maybe this is fate's way of repaying us for all the bad shit we've been through."

155

"Says the girl who thought fate was a load of bull just a few months ago."

"What can I say?" I shrugged as the elevator dinged. I leaned toward him, trailing my fingers up his torso, taking my time as I savored the feeling of the taut muscles that lay beneath his button-down shirt. His chest heaved in response to my touch. I swiftly grabbed his tie, tugging him into the elevator car, my gaze trained on him as I walked backwards, stopping when I hit the wall. "You made me a believer," I finished just as the doors closed, leaving us completely alone.

His lips curved as a feral look clouded his eyes. He gripped my wrist, forcing me to let go of his tie. Before I could say a word, he brought my body against his...hard, fast, desperate. I gasped, a tremor snaking through me as he lowered his head toward my neck. His tongue met my skin, his motions demanding, powerful, aggressive, but endearing at the same time. He held me as if he would never let go. He inhaled my scent as if he'd searched for months for the aroma. He tasted my skin as if it were the only thing that could quench his thirst.

My eyes fluttered into the back of my head, a tiny moan escaping as I curved into him, desperate to feel even more of him. I didn't care that we were in an elevator that still hadn't started moving. I wanted...no, *needed* this man now.

Suddenly, Dante released his hold on me and stepped back. I flung my eyes open to see a salacious, sly smile building on his mouth. With a wink, he turned from me, completely oblivious to the panting mess he'd turned me into. Or perhaps this was all part of his game. If there was one thing I'd learned about Dante, he loved the anticipation. And as frustrating as it was, I loved it, too. It made the end result all that more satisfying.

He fished a keycard out of his wallet, then inserted it into a slot in the panel. Once he pressed the button for the fourteenth floor, he spun back around, the sudden movement causing me to straighten in surprise. His heated gaze raked over every inch of my body as he loomed over me. The way he looked at me always made me feel raw and exposed, like he was peering into my soul. Tonight was no different. But for once, I wanted him to see everything, to know all of me. I wanted him to see the heartache I'd struggled with over the past few months. The regret that constantly plagued me as I considered whether I'd made the right decision in leaving him. The frustration that had pervaded my life as I tried to do everything in my power to stand on my own two feet so we could finally find our way back to each other.

"Kiss me, Dante," I begged softly as his mouth inched closer and closer to mine, but remained just out of reach.

"With pleasure, Eleanor."

Each second that passed as he slowly lowered his lips seemed to stretch, every part of me tingling with need, the anticipation unraveling any composure I had. Finally, our lips met. I sighed into him, his kiss the only thing in my life that felt right, his arms the only place that had ever felt like home.

Deepening the kiss, I raked my hands up his chest, tugging him harder into me. He groaned, his hands falling to my hips. Not caring about where we were or who could see us, he lifted me, hiking the skirt of my dress up as he pressed me against the elevator wall, thrusting between my legs.

"Dante," I moaned, throwing my head back as his lips trailed a fiery path down my neck, his fingers grazing my breasts. His light touch was at complete odds with the ravenous and greedy way he kissed me. It erased all thoughts regarding the complications that could potentially jeopardize a relationship between us. My father. His father. The distance. The lies. The secrets. All that had disappeared from my mind. All that mattered was this moment. And at this moment, I needed Dante. On my skin. Over my body. In my heart.

The elevator slowed to a stop and he reluctantly helped me lower my legs to the floor, leaving a deep, quick kiss on my lips. Once the doors opened, he grabbed my hand, leading me down a long corridor before coming to a stop in front of a door toward the end of the hallway. He removed his keycard and inserted it, unlocking the door. He opened it, standing back to allow me to enter in front of him.

Any other time, I would have taken a moment to admire the opulence and comfort surrounding me in the luxurious suite that probably cost more per night than I made in a month. I didn't care about the breathtaking view of the Hollywood Hills outside the balcony, or the oversized hot tub, or the bottle of champagne sitting on the wet bar. Dante loved foreplay, but there was a place and time for that. That place was not here, and the time was not now. Not after so long.

The door clicked behind him, the loud echo amplified by the anticipation inside me. I spun around, my eyes narrowed on him with an insatiable hunger. Not a word was spoken as I stepped out of my shoes and sauntered toward him, doing my best not to limp. I gingerly raised myself onto my toes, taking his earlobe between my teeth, nibbling and pulling.

"Fuck me, Dante," I murmured, my voice raspy and low, seductive. His breath hitched and he crushed my body against his.

"What happened to the Eleanor I met on a plane to Rome?" he asked coyly, brushing my hair over my shoulder. "The Eleanor who couldn't even look in my eyes when I asked her what she liked and didn't like in the bedroom?" He leaned closer, his two-day scruff rubbing against my neck. "The Eleanor who turned a bright shade of red when I asked her if she touched herself?" He pulled back, gazing down at me with a salacious smile.

"Thanks to you, that Eleanor is gone," I answered in an even tone. "I know what I like, what I don't. I know what I want. And right now, I want you to fuck me, to give me every reason to never walk away from you again. To remind me exactly of what I'll be missing if I do." I leaned in, running my tongue against his jawline, then took his earlobe between my teeth, tugging. "To claim me as yours."

Growling, he gripped my hair, yanking my head back. The sudden movement made me yelp. I breathed through the ache, my need for him only increasing with each second that passed. He dragged his lips across my neck, his teeth lightly grazing my skin.

"Harder," I begged as raw need filled me.

He loosened his grip on my hair and I met his conflicted eyes. "Are you sure? I don't—"

I pressed a finger to his lips, hushing him. "Shh. I love you, Dante. And I know you love me. I know you need this. I need this, too. I don't want to be in a relationship where sex is the same every single time. I want you to fuck me with reckless abandon, then pull me into your arms and whisper the most endearing and loving things in my ear as you give me that love. I want you to mark me, to see that wild look that comes over you as you drive harder and deeper than you ever have before. Then I want to feel your soft kisses as your lips feather across my shoulder blades, your touch barely there." I reached up, running my fingers down the line of his brow, cupping his cheek. "I want you to grip my head harder as your cock grows bigger and bigger in my mouth, making me take every single inch of you." I pressed a soft kiss against his lips, biting the bottom one. "Then I want you to brush the hair away from my eyes as we lay next to each other, your voice murmuring how much you love me the last thing I hear before I drift off to sleep."

I stepped back, lowering the zipper of my dress and allowing it to pool at my feet. "I love you, Dante, and that means every side of you. I love the dominating man who takes what he wants when he wants it. I love the sweet man who begged me with everything he had to stay, to not give up on us." I approached him, grabbing the lapels of his suit jacket, tugging it off his shoulders. "I never have, and I never will."

When I reached for his tie, about to loosen it, he clutched my forearm with a power I wasn't quite expecting. His eyes burning with raw need, his chest heaved as he stared at me in the simple nude bra and matching panties I wore. When I dressed for work today, I didn't exactly plan on ending my evening in a luxurious suite with Dante. Otherwise, I would have picked out different underwear.

He palmed my back, our bodies colliding. I could feel his erection twitching against my stomach. "God, I've missed you, *mia cara*." His hand roamed from my back to my side, trailing the line of my panties, his fingers brushing against my thighs. Pressing my lips to his, I ran my hands through his hair, tugging and pulling at it, making no attempt to be remotely gentle. "And it appears you've missed me quite a bit, too, haven't you?"

He grazed my panties, my wetness building more than it already had. Lifting the material, his finger ghosted against my heat. I panted, grabbing his wrist and forcing his hand farther between my legs.

"Don't tease, Dante. It's been too long."

"Whenever you pleasured yourself over the past few weeks, did you think of my fingers touching your swollen clit?" he murmured, his lips lingering on my neck.

"Yes," I squeaked out, spreading my legs slightly to give him better access. I was instantly reminded of our visit to the tea room at the foot of the Spanish Steps when he nearly drove me to orgasm at our table with just the brush of his fingers against me. It was remarkable how far we'd come since that day, that time, that place. Back then, I fully intended to have a one-night stand, then never see him again. But fate knew differently. She knew Dante was exactly what I needed in my life. And perhaps I was exactly what Dante needed in his.

"What else did you think about?"

"Your fingers plunging inside me."

"Like this?" He toyed with my folds, my breathing increasing, then pushed a finger inside.

I threw my head back as sparks ignited. My legs weakened. I struggled to maintain my balance as I slowly became unhinged with every thrust of his fingers.

"What else?" His body tightened, his jaw clenching.

"You taking me from behind," I panted as my eyes fluttered into the back of my head. I'd lost all control of my body and mind, a puppet to Dante's touch.

Instantly, he removed his fingers from inside me and spun me around, forcing my stomach against the back of the couch. He yanked my panties down my legs, anticipation bubbling in my core as I lay completely exposed to him. Yet it made me feel powerful, safe, strong.

His hands brushed between my thighs, running my

wetness all over me. I moaned, pulsing against him. I spent the past three months aching for this man's touch, his body, his love. I imagined his husky voice murmuring all the sensual and erotic things he wanted to do to me. I'd craved that feeling of euphoria only he could give me. Now that he was here, that he was mine, I was desperate for him in every way imaginable. I wanted to lose myself in him, to drown in his waters, to burn in his flame.

"Do you like that, Eleanor?" He fisted my hair, tugging my head back.

"More."

He leaned over me, his rough chin scraping against my shoulder blades. "Beg for me, Eleanor."

If I was turned on before, it was nothing compared to now, hearing his demanding voice become gruff, his grip on me tightening, marking me, possessing me…consuming me.

"Please, Dante," I said through my heavy breaths. "I need you to fuck me."

A hiss escaped his lips, followed by the sound of his belt coming undone. I tried to reel in all the sensations flowing through me when he pressed himself to me, his erection rubbing against my backside.

"God, I want to fuck you so bad right now," he growled, his lips on my neck, his hands roaming my body. "I've thought about little else over the past few months, about when I'd feel this perfect pink pussy clench around me as I drive inside you."

"Then what are you waiting for?" I panted,

unhinged. I ached to feel him, for him to fill me in a way no other man ever had, in a way no one would ever be able to again.

"For you to reach your breaking point," he whispered into my ear. "And you're not quite there yet." He nipped my neck, then stepped back, a chill washing over me from his absence.

"Seriously?!" I exclaimed, pushing off the couch, whirling around, my eyes on fire. "Even if you don't win for Outstanding Informational Series, you'll win the Eleanor for Biggest Tease in the Bedroom."

Grinning, he approached, his lips feathering against mine. "That's the only award I'm interested in." He paused. "Actually, that's not entirely true. I'm more interested in winning the Eleanor for Best Orgasm Ever."

I drew in a quick breath as his hands skimmed the cup of my bra, the only article of clothing that remained. I reached behind me and unhooked it, tossing it to the floor.

"Then come and get it." Turning from him, I sauntered toward the bedroom, glancing over my shoulder with a come-hither stare.

His eyes hooding with a devious look, he stalked across the living room, shrugging out of his shirt and tie as he made his way toward me. He wrapped his arms around my waist, pulling me against him.

"For your consideration, *signorina*…"

Before I could respond, he crushed his lips to mine, his kiss bruising as he gave me every last part of himself, and I him.

"Get on the bed," he instructed as he pulled away, his tone harsh. "On your hands and knees, facing the headboard. And spread your legs."

I looked into his dark eyes, which gave nothing away, my voice caught in my throat.

"Now," he barked, squeezing my ass roughly, then stepped away from me. His stance was wide, his arms crossed in front of his broad chest, his stare formidable.

My stomach fluttering, I followed his demands, positioning myself on my hands and knees, staring at the headboard. Silence filled the room. I expected to feel Dante behind me, but didn't. I was so tempted to glanced over my shoulder, to see what he was doing, to take in his beautiful toned body. Instead, I focused on my surroundings...the beside lamp, the cushioned headboard, the framed black-and-white print of downtown LA, the Capitol Records building prominent. This reminded me of our first night together when I was in this exact position on his bed, staring at the painting overhead. I was a different woman back then. I marveled at how much I'd changed in just three months.

When I felt the bed dip, I instinctively glanced over my shoulder at Dante's now naked frame.

"Face forward," he ordered.

I quickly followed his demand, feeling as if my heart were going to burst through the walls of my chest at any moment. I'd never been so turned on before. The unknown. The uncertainty. The unrelenting need. It overpowered everything else.

I felt the heat of his chest hovering over my back, the hair on my nape standing on end. Then he slipped a mask over my eyes, shrouding my world in darkness.

"All my international flying has paid off. I knew I could put these eye masks to better use one of these days."

A tremble rolled down my spine, following the line his finger drew. Unable to see, every other sense was heightened. Smell. Sound. Feel. Oh god, the feel of this man as the heat from his chest danced so close to my skin would unravel me. I feared the instant he pushed inside me, it would be game over. I'd be the welcome recipient of one of the most mind-altering, earth-shattering orgasms. It would be one for the history books. An orgasm to put all other orgasms to shame.

His hands gripped the back of my thighs briefly before loosening their hold, one of his fingers teasing me. I moaned, moving into him, trying to signal with my body what I wanted, what I needed.

"Mmm... So greedy."

"Dante," I begged. I didn't know how much more of this I could take, but I would have been lying if I said I wasn't enjoying every delicious, spine-tingling second of waiting, of pining, of lusting.

He trailed his finger from my center, up the curve of my backside, and down again. Over. And over. And over. Repeating. Teasing. Torturing. Suddenly, there was nothing. No rush of desire from his hands on me. No heat of his body near mine. No whisper of his carnal thoughts as I lay completely exposed to him.

The bed shifted and dipped as a warmth settled close to my thighs. I would have given anything to yank this eye mask off, to see what Dante was doing, where he was, but I resisted the urge, the unknown heightening every single sensation flowing through me.

"Spread your legs wider, Eleanor," he said, his hands gripping my thighs. "And put your weight on your elbows."

I did as he requested, my chest heaving as I placed my forearms on the mattress, the heat of Dante close to my core growing stronger. Then his mouth was on me, his tongue swirling, licking, tasting.

"Fuck," I breathed out, clenching my hands into fists, grabbing onto the sheets. I soared as he circled me, devoured me, consumed me. This man. This beautiful, passionate man. How had I survived the past three months without his touch, without his heart, without his love? I never wanted to be without him again. I never wanted to stop feeling this all-consuming spark of electricity that flowed through me as I climbed higher, higher, higher, fireworks erupting before my eyes, in my body, in my heart as I screamed out his name, coming undone.

But he didn't stop. He kept teasing me, sucking and licking, inserting a finger, then two, as I still struggled to come down from my first orgasm. And that was Dante's plan. He didn't want me to come down. He wanted me to stay in the clouds, with him, where we belonged. With each flick of his tongue, each thrust of his fingers, each murmur of his voice, he catapulted me even higher than I'd been before, orgasm after orgasm rolling through me to the point where I didn't know when one ended and the other began.

"I can't…," I struggled to say. Even if I didn't have the mask covering my eyes, I was certain my world would have been dark, unable to see through the flashes before me. "It's so good, but I don't think my body can handle any more."

It didn't matter that I couldn't see his face. I could feel the smirk crawling across his lips. "No more?" he mused as the bed shifted. His hand lighted against my back, then he grabbed my hips, forcing me into him, teasing me. "Are you sure about that, Eleanor?"

I whimpered, words escaping me, his erection pulsing against me. "No," I said finally, finding my voice. "Let me feel you."

"Did you not just feel me?" he mused coyly, torturing me, wetting his tip with my arousal. My muscles clenched, aching for him to fill me, to give me all of him.

"You know what I mean, Dante. I want you inside me."

"Were my fingers not enough?"

I groaned in frustration. God, this man was exasperating, but I loved it. And he knew that. He knew exactly what I needed, what I craved, what would bring me more pleasure than anything ever had.

"I want your cock, Dante." My voice became firm, resolute. "Now!"

Without a moment's hesitation, he thrust into me, both of us letting out a satisfied moan, relief seeming to wash over our bodies as we found our rhythm. He wrapped an arm around my waist, supporting me, leaning over and nipping on my skin.

"Don't ever walk away from me again, Eleanor." His demanding voice turned pleading, desperate, sincere. "I don't ever want to spend another day without you." He gripped my wrists, his body covering mine. "Say you're mine."

"I'm yours," I murmured.

Truer words had never been spoken. I was his in every sense of the word. He'd consumed all my thoughts since I'd met him. He possessed my heart, something no one else had ever been able to do. He reinvigorated my soul, breathing life back into me, showing me what it was like to really live, to love…to fly. I needed him just as much as he needed me. It didn't make sense, but I no longer cared what was rational and practical. All I cared about was feeling the love I used to think was a myth, the love Dante had for me and I for him.

"And I'm yours," he replied. "*Sempre e per sempre.*"

"*Sempre e per sempre,*" I repeated, my body quivering as an orgasm overtook me.

Dante leaned back, pulling out of me, then quickly flipped me over, removing the eye mask.

"I was enjoying that," I said through my heavy breaths, my body still tingling.

"I need to see your eyes, Eleanor. I had to go months

169

without it. Never again." He pushed into me once more, his motions slow, measured, giving me every last piece of him, then withdrawing before repeating the same sensual rhythm. He leaned down, his gaze locked with mine as he held my head in his strong hands. "Never again."

"Never again," I breathed as I raked my fingers down his back, the feeling of my nails digging into his skin the final straw.

His eyes grew wide, bliss rolling over him as he fell to pieces, murmuring incantations of unending love. My heart swelled with gratitude that fate had given me this man exactly when I needed him. I used to think fate was something for the dreamers. But I believed now. Fate was real. It did exist. And this man shivering and trembling on top of me was proof of that.

Chapter Fourteen

N ARM SNAKED AROUND me as a dull morning light seeped into the plush bedroom, rousing me from a restful slumber. I let out a contented sigh. "I was worried it was a dream," I admitted, my voice raspy from sleep.

Dante kissed my shoulder blades, his hand firmly placed against my stomach, his embrace swallowing me. "It's not," he assured me, his lips grazing my skin, causing a shiver to run through me.

"Do you have any idea how many times I dreamed that you found me, only to wake up and learn it wasn't real?"

"It's real, *mia cara*. I'm here. And I'm not leaving your side." He pushed me onto my back and I opened my eyes, meeting his gaze. "You're going to get so sick of me you'll wish I was still halfway around the world."

I laughed, running my fingers through his hair, lifting my mouth to meet his. "Impossible. I'm never letting you go again."

His lips gently brushed against mine, his motions sweet and almost reserved as his hands ran along the contours of my body, a complete one-eighty from the carnal, dominating lover he was last night. I ran my fingers down his sculpted back, wrapping my legs around his waist. I couldn't get enough of him. I never wanted to leave this bed, never wanted to be apart from this man, never wanted to stop feeling his skin on mine.

He dragged his tongue along my jawbone, nipping on my neck before slithering down the length of my body, not leaving an inch of me undiscovered. Every dip. Every curve. Every valley. He treasured and explored each of them, loving each imperfection in a way that made me fall for him even more.

"Your skin is so soft, Eleanor," he crooned. His rough hands ran across my hipbone, his lips following the path his fingers set. "So silky. So perfect."

He propped himself on his knees, my legs falling on either side of him. Gripping my hips, he pulled me toward him and positioned himself between my thighs. He took his time, slowly entering me, then withdrawing before pushing into me again. His motions were so languid, so gentle, so delicate...so perfect. No other word could describe the way he moved inside me, giving me everything he had, filling me to the hilt, then lovingly retreating before repeating the same sensual motion.

"Dante," I moaned, moving with his rhythm. "God, I love you. I love this. I just..." Opening my eyes, I grabbed his face in my hands, peering into his dark pools that were filled with a thousand emotions — reverence, hunger, unabashed adoration. "I love you so much it hurts," I said with a quiver. "Without you..."

He blew out a breath, resting his forehead on mine, maintaining his delicate rhythm. "I know, *amore mio*. I know. But I'm here. I'm all yours. We'll never have to experience that emptiness again."

"Promise?" I asked, wrapping my arms tighter around him, even a breath between us too much distance. "I can't lose you again."

"Never again. Promise." He hooked his arm around my waist, rolling onto his back and bringing me on top of him.

I took a moment to acclimate myself, then moved against him, shading his face with my hair. He reached up, running his hands through it, our eyes glued to each other. The intensity, the connection, the passion was immeasurable as we savored in this love we shared. This love most people searched their entire life for. This love I would never again take for granted.

"Come on, baby." He brought my lips to his. "I want to see you come," he murmured against my mouth, his grip on my hips tightening as he increased his motions, lifting me off him, then slamming me back down.

I gasped, my breathing increasing with each thrust.

"You like that?"

I leaned back, every muscle in my body clenching as he lifted me again, then forced me back onto him, harder, more punishing.

"Dante," I moaned, closing my eyes, a slave to the sensation. His finger found my clit and I cried out again, falling on top of him, a wave of unmatched euphoria washing over me as I came undone. He continued thrusting into me, then let out a strangled groan when he found his own release.

"God, I love being inside you," he murmured, his voice husky with need. "There is nothing like it in the world." He crushed his mouth against mine, our kiss greedy as we struggled to catch our breath. "And I've been to some remarkable places," he finished with a smile.

"I quite like when you're inside me, too." I slowly circled my hips against him, making him groan.

"You're a tiger."

I giggled, rolling off him, about to get out of the bed. "Just trying to make up for lost time."

He pulled me back against him. "Don't go clean up yet," he begged. "We'll shower together in a minute. I just want to feel you in my arms right now."

Sighing, I snuggled my head against his chest. How could I deny him when he said such sweet things? I rested my arm across his torso and listened to his heartbeat, wanting to thank God, fate, destiny, whoever for finally reuniting us.

"How did you find me last night?" I asked, breaking through the silence as I toyed with the few tuffs of hair on his chest. "I knew where you would be, but despite all my efforts in getting to you, fate pushed back."

He looked down at me. "So you said. What happened?"

"Traffic."

"That's not unusual."

"No. But it was certainly worse than normal, even for a Friday night. I'd finally had it and was close enough that I decided to get off by the Staples Center. When I was five blocks away, there was a street barricaded because of filming or something. Then, of course, there was a ton of heavy traffic because of the road closures. When I finally got close, I knew there wouldn't be any parking, so I left my car in a tow zone. I started running toward campus, but my heel got caught and I twisted my ankle. Still, it was all for nothing. By the time I made it to the theater, you were gone...or so I thought."

He grabbed my chin and forced my gaze to his. "Maybe it was all fate's plan. Maybe she just wanted to know that you would fight for us, despite any obstacle we faced."

I peered into his eyes, responding with the only thing I could. "I'll always fight for you. Now that I know how miserable my life is without you in it, I'll gladly suffer through a towed car, twisted ankle, and anything else to be with you."

A breathtaking smile crossed his face. "That makes me very happy to hear." He placed a gentle kiss on my lips, then pulled back.

It was silent for a moment, then I asked, "How did you know I'd be at the Rose Garden?"

"I didn't." He ran his hand up and down my back, tracing different patterns on my skin. "We got caught in that same street blockade as you. My driver decided to backtrack and get on the freeway by the Colosseum. You can imagine my surprise when I saw someone who looked like you duck into the Rose Garden. I almost didn't tell him to stop. I figured my brain was just playing tricks on me, like it had been the past several months." He cupped my cheeks, his eyes growing intense.

"I saw you everywhere, too, Eleanor. You were the waitress at every restaurant. You were the flight attendant mixing my drinks on the plane. You were the woman at the airport rushing to hug the lucky bastard behind me who'd just gotten back home." He shook his head, exhaling a small breath. "But something about last night, about this feeling inside me, made me tell my driver to let me out and go on without me so I could see for myself." He lowered his mouth to mine. "And I'm so glad I did."

I sighed, melting further into him, throwing my leg over his waist. I could stay in this spot all day.

"Do you have any big plans this weekend?" he asked after a few moments, still playing with my hair.

"Not really." I stared at the disheveled sheets and the trail of clothes leading from the bedroom into the living room, all a happy reminder of last night…and this morning. "Other than the typical Sunday brunch at Mila's." I lifted my head, peering into his eyes. "It's always been a tradition with us, even when I was with Brock." My expression fell briefly before I recovered. "But today, I'm all yours."

"I want you to be all mine tomorrow, too."

I hesitated, pulling my lip between my teeth. "I guess I can tell Mila I can't make it."

"I'd never ask to come between you and your friend.

I want to go with you."

I furrowed my brow. "You do?"

"Like I told you in Italy, Eleanor, I want to be a part of your life, and I want you to be a part of mine. So, if you don't mind, I'd like to meet Mila."

"She has two kids," I said in warning. "It's not anything fancy. It's just our excuse to drink before noon on a Sunday."

"I don't need anything extravagant. As long as I'm with you, that's all that matters."

I studied him for a moment, then shrugged. "Okay then. It's a date, I guess."

"Speaking of dates…" He placed a kiss on my nose, then freed himself from my arms, rising from the bed. I sat up, admiring his backside as he strode across the room and took out a pair of boxer briefs from the dresser, pulling them on. "There's a little award show I'm scheduled to attend here in Los Angeles tomorrow evening. I'd be honored if you'd accompany me."

My eyes widened. "Dante, I…" I shook my head. "I'd love to, but I don't have a dress appropriate to wear to any red-carpet event. Or the money to buy a new one. I've only been at my new job a month, and it doesn't pay nearly close to what my last one did. I'm still paying off my credit card, and after bills and all that… Not to mention it would be next to impossible to—"

"It's a good thing I planned ahead then, isn't it?" he interrupted, a devilish grin on his face.

He opened the closet, revealing the dress I wore to

the gala at the art exhibit back in June, cleaned, pressed, and ready to be worn. My jaw dropped, confusion crossing my brow as my gaze floated between Dante and the dress. He walked to me, pressing a soft kiss on my nose.

"I had no intention of leaving the city without you promising to be mine, Eleanor," he explained, answering the question that was readily apparent on my face.

"God, I love you." I pulled him on top of me, kissing him deeply. The fact he was willing to fight just as hard for me endeared another piece of my heart to him.

"I'll never tire of hearing you tell me that."

I hooked my fingers in his boxer briefs and pushed them down his legs, a sigh of appreciation escaping my throat when he slid into me again. He flexed his hips toward me, then withdrew slowly, letting me feel every inch of him.

I lost myself in him once more, forgetting about reality for one more day, one more hour, one more minute, thinking about nothing but the happiness I felt in our bubble. Dante and I met in the clouds, we fell in love in the clouds. Would our love be strong enough to survive the return to earth? I had to believe it would. I had to believe fate wouldn't give me a taste, give *us* a taste, just to rip it all away again.

As we lay on the bed in the aftermath of our lovemaking, our appendages a tangle of arms and legs, moments away from sleep, a loud clap of thunder rang through the room and I startled.

Dante pulled me closer, kissing the top of my head, soothing me as I looked out the window at the heavy clouds rolling over the city. "Shh," he mumbled drowsily. "No one will take you away."

I snapped my eyes back to his, wondering what he meant by that. Hearing his even breathing, I figured he was just dreaming. But that didn't stop a chill from washing over me as I turned to stare at the darkening sky, his words repeating in my head. Somewhere in the recesses of my mind, my memories, I knew he meant them, that he wasn't just talking in his sleep, that there was a reason he uttered them.

A streak of lightning flashed in the early morning light, unsettling me, the weather uncharacteristic for this time of year. My stomach rolled, my body shivering despite the warmth coming off Dante.

A storm was coming…

PLAYLIST

Won't You Come Again - Susie Suh

In My Dreams - Ruth B.

Over and Over - Rachael Yamagata

I Walk a Little Faster - Fiona Apple

Don't Let Me Down - Joy Williams

Basket Case - Sara Bareilles

Since You've Been Around - Rosie Thomas

Drink You Gone - Ingrid Michaelson

A Little Bit - Tristan Prettyman

I Am Here - P!nk

All Again - Elle Henderson

1,000 Years - Liza Ann

Northern Sky - Nick Drake

Chainsmoking - Jacob Banks

All On My Mind - Anderson East

Bright Lights and Cityscapes - Sara Bareilles

INFERNO: PART 4

He found me in the dark when I thought all hope was lost.

He swore he loved me when I didn't think anyone ever would.

He vowed to keep the shadows haunting me at bay when I felt like I was drowning in my past. But in doing so, he also kept the truth from me.

It shouldn't surprise me. After all, our relationship was built on a foundation of lies, the walls constructed of secrets, the roof a thin veil of deceit.

But as I start to peel away layer after layer of this wasps nest I find myself entangled in, I'm faced with the truth…*our* truth.

A truth even the strongest love can't protect us from.

A truth that's been staring at me for years, but I've simply been too blind to see it.

A truth that's about to destroy everything.

Acknowledgements

I've always been a sucker for classic movies. If you've been an avid reader of mine, you've probably picked up on that, due to my mention of some of my favorites — *Casablanca*, *To Have and Have Not*, *An Affair to Remember*, just to name a few. One of my absolute favorites has always been *Roman Holiday*. It's such a sweet, fun story about two people who shouldn't be together falling for each other, set against the backdrop of one of the most beautiful cities in the world — Rome. I've always wondered what happened after Joe Bradley walked away from Princess Ann at the press conference, where she learned exactly who he was. Thus *Inferno* was born.

Of course, when I first set out to write this story, I had no intention of exploring that question. My intention was to write a short, sexy, sinful story of a woman escaping to Rome, just like Princess Ann did. Much like in *Roman Holiday*, I thought my story would end with Eleanor walking away from Dante, grateful that he'd opened her eyes to what life could be when she allowed herself to forget about her responsibilities for a short period of time. Never did I anticipate exploring what could have happened after they went their separate ways. I've always wondered if Princess Ann and Joe Bradley found their way back to each other. And I'd like to think they would, that if they were truly meant to be together, fate would have made it so…just like fate's had a hand in Dante and Eleanor's story from the very beginning.

This has become one of my favorite stories to date, and I think it's because I've made fate such a big part of this plot. We all like to believe in fate, in hope, in love. We all like to believe that even when things suck, there's a reason for that, that the clouds will eventually part and the sun will shine again.

So first, I need to thank the reason I believe in fate, my wonderful husband, Stan, and the always adorable Harper Leigh. I'm truly blessed to have such a supportive husband and a daughter who makes me smile even when she's throwing a tantrum. (Hello terrible twos!)

On that note, a huge thanks to my two nannies, Sharon and Brooke, for watching Harper so I have time to write.

When I first started this project, it was just supposed to be one book. Then it morphed into two. Then three. Then four. All along the way, my editor, Kim Young, was flexible, adapting to the changing storyline as this plot grew into the complex tale it is now. She's the only one I'd ever trust with my manuscripts and I couldn't do this without her eyes and brain.

Another big thanks to Laura Rossi for making sure all my Italian is correct.

To my beta team — Lin, Melissa, Joelle, Sylvia, Stacy, Victoria — Burnham Bitches for Life. Or should we be saying Italians Do It Better? #AlexanderWho

To my street team, thank you for all your help in promoting me. To my reader group, thanks for giving me a place to go when I need a break from writing. I love interacting with you about books or whatever else pops into our heads. To all the ladies at Social Butterfly PR, especially Emily, thanks for agreeing to take on this insane project and for keeping me on track and organized.

Last but not least, thank you to all you wonderful readers! Thanks for picking up my book. Thank you for falling in love with my characters. On behalf of all authors, thank you for reading.

I can't wait to share the finale of Dante and Eleanor's story with all of you. A storm is coming!

Peace and love,

~ T.K.

BOOKS BY T.K. LEIGH

The Beautiful Mess Series
A Beautiful Mess
A Tragic Wreck
Gorgeous Chaos

The Deception Duet
Chasing The Dragon
Slaying The Dragon

The Vault
Inferno

Stand Alone Titles
Heart Of Light
Heart Of Marley
The Other Side Of Someday
Vanished
Writing Mr. Right

For more information on any of these titles and
upcoming releases, please visit T.K.'s website:
www.tkleighauthor.com

ABOUT THE AUTHOR

T.K. Leigh, otherwise known as Tracy Leigh Kellam, is the *USA Today* Bestselling author of the Beautiful Mess series, in addition to several other works. Originally from New England, she now resides in sunny Southern California with her husband, beautiful daughter, and three cats. When she's not planted in front of her computer, writing away, she can be found training for her next marathon (of which she has run over twenty fulls and far too many halfs to recall) or chasing her daughter around the house.

T.K. Leigh is represented by Jane Dystel of Dystel, Goderich & Bourret Literary Management. All publishing inquiries, including audio, foreign, and film rights, should be directed to her.

Made in the USA
Columbia, SC
24 April 2018